MW00399489

Tales of the Were
Grizzly Cove

The Bear's
Healing Touch

BIANCA D'ARC

This book is a work of fiction. The names, characters, places, and incidents are products of the writer's imagination or have been used fictitiously and are not to be construed as real. Any resemblance to persons, living or dead, actual events, locale or organizations is entirely coincidental.

No part of this book may be used or reproduced in any manner whatsoever without written permission, except in the case of brief quotations embodied in critical articles and reviews.

DEDICATION

As all my work, this book is dedicated to my family, first and foremost. I would never have been able to follow my dream of writing if not for the support and encouragement of my parents, who taught me to reach for the stars.

I'd also like to thank my editor, Jess, and my good friend, Peggy, for assisting with making this a better, cleaner and hopefully, more enjoyable story. Thanks also to all the readers who have stuck with me over the years. You guys are the best!

CHAPTER ONE

Sirena hated being laid up and out of the action. Her people needed her, and she was stuck in bed, too hurt to move. Damned sea monster had nearly killed her, and only her hunting party's fast action and the timely arrival of a werebear, who had more than his share of chutzpa and magical ability, had allowed her to continue living. He'd saved her life and the lives of every member of her pod.

And then, he'd brought them all to safety in the sheltered waters of Grizzly Cove. It all seemed almost too good to be true...except for one thing. Or rather, one *man*.

The lone doctor in this small community

had patched her up, certainly, but he was also driving her completely insane. He was some kind of giant bear shifter who looked at her in ways that made her uncomfortable…and very aware of her femininity. That wasn't something she was used to in the hunting party. Her life in the sea, these past years, had been very different than how she had lived on land, and being around the handsome doctor brought that fact home.

The rest of the people who came in and out of his office—which had a private hospital-style room that she was currently inhabiting while she recovered—seemed to like him well enough. She could hear a lot of what happened out in the main area when the door was ajar. He seemed to be pleasant to most of the visitors who came by to get supplies or just chat with the doctor.

He didn't have a lot of patients because the town was full of shifters and they healed fast. As did mer—when they hadn't been sliced and diced in a zillion different ways and dragged out of the water more than half dead.

That's the pathetic state Sirena had been in when her pod had brought her ashore and put her into the doctor bear's hands. He'd had to stitch her together in a few places because her energy reserves were so low she couldn't heal even the small cuts. All her healing magic had been going toward just keeping herself alive in the beginning, and she'd been drained to the point where she was recovering at a much slower rate than normal.

The good news, of course, was that she was recovering at all. She probably should have died of her injuries, but her people—and the doctor—had saved her. The bad news was that her energy was still at an all-time low. She was healing, but slowly. At something like a human pace rather than a mer level. And it was infuriating.

Sirena wanted to be better *now*. She wanted to be out there in the town, making sure her people were safe and helping to organize things. After all, the Alpha bear of the Clan, who had set up this town, had invited the mer here and given them safe harbor from the creature and its minions that were out there in the ocean, preying on magical folk. The creatures that had nearly killed her. The leviathan. And all its evil little friends.

They were things of legend, not of this world. Creatures of evil that consumed magical folk and swallowed their souls. A terror she never wanted to meet again.

She'd been traumatized enough the first time, and almost hadn't lived through the encounter. And she'd only been chomped on by one of the smaller sea monsters that were somehow connected magically to the largest one—the one that led them all and had been brought through the rift from the forgotten realms to which they had been banished long ago. They seemed to travel and hunt as a group, the leviathan directing the movements of its smaller companions.

They were from another realm where magic abounded and they all fed on magic. At least, that's what the bears thought. She'd asked many questions since coming to Grizzly Cove and being stuck in their clinic. There wasn't much else she could do right now except talk, so she welcomed the times when her friends came to visit and pass on news of the things they'd learned about the creatures.

But she didn't want to think about it anymore. Not right now, when frustration was riding her hard. Of course, all she did lately was lie in bed and think. It was all too much. Sirena was a woman of action. As the leader of a hunting party of mer, she decided where they would go, what they would hunt, and when they would return to the larger group that counted on them to provide food and protection from the threats of the ocean.

To look at her now, no one would ever realize that she was a warrior. One of the mer's best. No, now, she was a weakling. An invalid. Stuck in bed, for the most part, needing help with the most basic necessities of life. Someone had to bring her food. Someone had to help her get up when she needed to limp over to the attached bathroom. Someone had to administer painkillers, just so she could sleep. It was unheard of. Mer didn't feel pain away humans did. Not often, anyway.

Circumstances had to be pretty bad for a mer of Sirena's caliber and experience to be laid so low. And they had been. She had gone toe to toe with a real-life sea monster and lost. It was a crushing blow to her pride, but the encounter also had damaged her courage.

She now had nightmares—for the first time in her life. They were all about the leviathan and its minions—and the rows of razor sharp teeth that had savaged her skin and broken her body. She woke in a cold sweat every night, at least once, reliving the terrible moments when she'd thought for certain she was going to die.

Sirena hated feeling weak. She should be stronger than this, dammit! She shouldn't be ready to leap out of her skin at the slightest sound and jump at every shadow.

But she was. And she hated it. She hated herself.

She hated the bear shifter doctor most of all, for reminding her of her own weakness. And for seeing her at her worst.

Oh, he was a handsome son of a gun, all right. Why couldn't she have met him when she was in her prime, instead of broken down and nearly crippled? Surely the Goddess was punishing her for her vanity to show her what might have been with a man who could very well be Sirena's equal.

It was obvious that he was a bear to be reckoned with, and his fellows treated him with cautious courtesy, except for the inner circle that dared treat him as an equal. That small group, she had come to learn, was the core group of ex-Special Forces bear shifter soldiers who followed the Alpha of the colony, John Marshall.

They didn't follow him blindly, though. Bears weren't like other kinds of shifters in that respect. They were mostly solitary beings, and this group had decided to band together as a sort of social experiment when the small unit of soldiers had decided to leave the armed forces behind. John had bought up the land, being the acknowledged strategist of the group, and had laid out his plan, hoping his friends would follow his lead.

They had, and almost overnight, the new town of Grizzly Cove had been born.

They'd put out the call through shifter networks for other bear shifters, hoping to attract females so the single men could find mates. What they'd attracted was trouble, in the form of the leviathan and its friends, that had been drawn—near as anyone could figure—to the concentration of bear shifter magic on this part of the Washington coast.

Bears were among the most magical of shifters. There weren't a lot of them, and they'd never really gathered in such numbers before. So maybe that's why the leviathan—a creature that devoured magic—had been drawn here.

Once they'd realized the problem, the bear shifters had begun to work on it. They'd achieved a no-go zone for the evil creatures inside the sheltered cove, but just beyond the beach, the leviathan and its minions lay in wait for any creature foolish enough to venture too near.

As a result, the mer had relocated to the cove, for the time being, at the invitation of the Alpha. Two of her friends had recently mated bear shifters, and it boded well for the unexpected compatibility of their species. Mer were shifters too...of a sort. But most mated with humans, or other mer, if they mated at all. This inter-species mating between bear shifters and mer was something new.

The mer had extensive networks on land, and they were bringing all their resources to bear on the town of Grizzly Cove. Sirena, as the leader of her hunting party and a member of the pod's leadership, should be out there, helping organize things. Instead, she was stuck in the clinic, feeling useless, with severely damaged pride and hurt feelings in addition to the scars she would bear for the rest of her life.

At least she was alive. That was something to be thankful for, but she lost sight of that during the tedious hours spent in bed, bored out of her mind.

"And how are we feeling today?" The deep voice of the bear shifter doctor came to her from the doorway of her prison cell-like room.

"*We* are just fine, doc," she told him, annoyed that she'd been so lost in thought he'd managed to sneak up on her. Again.

Her senses were really dulled here on land and especially since she'd been injured. Nobody had ever managed to surprise her before. Not in years, at least. And now, this bear shifter got the drop on her pretty much every time she encountered him. It was vastly annoying. Infuriating, even. She was losing her edge, and it was pissing her off.

"How's the pain level? Tolerable?" he asked, seemingly unfazed by her sarcastic tone.

"I'm fine," she repeated through clenched teeth. She loathed being so weak.

The doctor—all six feet seven inches of him—regarded her critically. He really was too damned handsome for his own good. Blond with icy blue eyes, he had that Nordic thing going on, with just a hint of Native American influence that showed in his tanned skin and high cheekbones.

"Let's just take a look at those dressings," he plowed on, moving closer as he flipped through papers on a chart he'd been keeping of her progress. She'd tried to read the little notations he'd made, but she couldn't make heads or tails of his abbreviations and codes.

Sirena was still swathed in bandages that had to be changed every day. The worst was around her midsection, where the creature had gotten hold of her and thrashed its head. She figured the evil thing had been intent on breaking her in two. Sawing her in half with its rows of teeth…or something equally sinister.

She held out her arm grudgingly. They'd settled into a routine where he did her arms first, then her legs, then saved the worst for last, checking out the wounds on her abdomen and back that wrapped all around her body. It wasn't pretty. She was sure of that.

For a male, he had a surprisingly gentle touch as he unrolled the gauze from around her forearm. The dressings on her arms had gotten smaller over the past few days, the skin gradually healing. When she looked at what he uncovered, she was pleased—and a bit surprised—to find only scabs left on what had been deep gashes on her right arm.

"I think we can leave this uncovered now," he said, surprising her again. Was she making progress? Slow-as-molasses progress, but still progress? Goddess be praised. "It's coming along nicely. How about the other one?"

Mutely, she held out her other arm, and he repeated the unwrapping procedure.

"Hmm. We can leave off the lower part, but that gash on your upper arm still needs a bit of protection. We can go with a smaller bandage though."

Putting actions to his words, he reached over to a supply drawer and pulled out a large adhesive bandage. He cleaned the area around the wound before applying the new dressing, working quietly and efficiently, as always.

He finished up there, then went to the foot of her bed and lifted up the sheet that covered her feet. He unwrapped her left foot, which had taken a direct hit on the instep that made walking not much fun. There was progress there too, which he rewarded with a smaller bandage, though she still felt a bit like a mummy. Her right foot was deemed in better shape, and he left off the wrappings, choosing a few large adhesive bandages instead.

He replaced the sheet over her feet and tucked it in gently, which was an odd gesture for such a manly man to make. She would have been touched, if she wasn't so mad about being banged up this bad.

"Lie back, Sirena," he said softly, coming to her side.

They'd worked out a system for this particular check over the past few days. She would lay flat, and he'd lift the gown to just below her breasts—the monster's teeth had nicked the bottom of one, which the doctor treated with the utmost circumspectness, only baring the skin he needed to see to work. He'd then lower the sheet to just below her hip bones.

The majority of the damage was to her midsection, front and back. He'd see to the front side first, then help her roll onto her side so he could examine the back. He'd put extra cushions under her to make the otherwise hard hospital bed softer on the shredded skin of her back. He had some kind of gel-filled cushions that kept her cool and comfortable, almost making her feel as if she was floating—which was especially comforting to her, considering she had spent at least half her life in the ocean.

His touch was healing, even if his eyes were hard. He never spoke much while he worked on her wounds, but as she'd started to regain her strength, little by little, he'd become a little more talkative. Not much, but a bit. He'd make the odd comment now and again, which was more than he'd done in the beginning.

"This is coming along. I think some of your magic is returning, but we'll have to talk to Gus or a priestess to be sure. I've always thought it was our innate magic that aids in our healing abilities. Whenever I've seen a shifter unable to heal normally, it's usually because he's expended a great deal of his magic and it needs time to rebuild. The creature was still feeding on you, Sirena." Those glacial blue eyes met hers, and she saw the outrage she experienced at those words reflected in his eyes. "But you weren't an easy victim for the monster. You fought back, and you lived to fight another day. Take heart in that."

It was as if he knew how bad she felt about needing to be rescued. Needing someone else to fight her battle with that cursed sea creature. She was a failure. A false leader. A fraud.

"Easy for you to say," she mumbled, turning away. She heard him sigh.

"How about you roll over so I can check your back? Any discomfort?" he asked as if he hadn't just reopened her worst emotional wound.

"My whole body is one big *discomfort*, doc. I feel awful," she admitted.

"But better than you were before, right?"

Grudgingly, she agreed as she sucked in a breath at the pain rolling to her side caused.

She felt his warm touch on her back, and just that touch eased the pain a little. He had magic in his fingers, this bear doctor.

CHAPTER TWO

She'd missed the touch of a man. She hadn't been with anyone since seeking the solace of the ocean five years ago. She'd had a man on shore before then, but he'd turned out to be a louse. A cheater who thought it was all right to sleep with her...and any other woman who caught his fancy.

Sirena had sought the peace of ocean life and hadn't gone back except to visit friends on the occasional holiday. She'd told them she was traveling—which wasn't a lie. Life under the waves was constant motion, constant going from one place to the other, seeking better fishing or calmer waters.

There weren't that many men in the

colony, and most of them were mated, raising young families. All in all, Sirena was happier without any male involvement in her life. Or so she'd thought.

But now, she was here, in the middle of Bear City, USA, where almost the entire population was male. Male bear shifters of various kinds. Most were grizzlies and black bears, but there were a few Kodiak bears, polar bears, some kind of giant Russian breed of bear, even two pandas and a koala, she'd been told. Although, she figured they were joking about the koala. And to be fair, the pandas were both female. A mother and daughter from China who had come into the office yesterday when the little girl had taken a bad tumble out of a stand of bamboo.

Sirena had seen the little girl named Daisy when she'd peeked into the room, curious as all six year olds. The mother, Lynn, had come after her and apologized for Daisy's curiosity, but Sirena hadn't minded at all. It had been something to break up her monotonous day.

Oh, members of her hunting party came to visit, but since she'd begun to stay awake more during the day, there were long hours filled with boredom. They'd hooked up a television for her, but other than the documentary channels, she wasn't really interested in human news or politics, and their entertainment was somewhat moronic when she knew what was waiting out there in the ocean. How could she laugh at some farcical comedy show when there was evil poised just off shore, looking for any opening to decimate the town and all its people?

The doctor's hands supported her as she began to slide backward, her strength ebbing quickly, as it had since her injury. Then, she felt him sit on the bed behind her, his muscular butt wedged up against hers, keeping her in place while he worked on her wounds.

"Sorry, ma'am," he said gently. "This'll just take a few minutes more. It would be better if we could get you off your back for a bit. Maybe you could sit up in a chair or even walk around a little, if you're feeling up to it. All this lying on your back is causing the wounds here to take longer to heal."

She wanted to cry. How was she going to stand when she couldn't be sure when her strength would give out? She'd felt reasonably stable until he'd asked her to roll over. She'd held the position for a few minutes, but then, the weakness had come, and she felt as shaky as a wet kitten. No stamina.

"Don't call me ma'am," she managed to grumble.

"No? Don't like that, eh?" the doc mused. "How about *Sirena?*" Her name sounded like a caress in his deep voice. "But I'll only call you by name if you'll do the same. I'm Sven."

"Sven? Seriously?" She almost laughed. "Next, you'll tell me you were a ski instructor or something."

"Ski Patrol, not instructor," he replied, sounding confused.

Sirena rolled her eyes. Of course he was some kind of Olympic skier. With a name like Sven, what else could he possibly be? Maybe a masseur? Now that idea brought up all kinds of naughty possibilities, but she ordered her mind to definitely *not* go there. Nope. No siree, Bob. Or Sven, as the case may be.

"I'm not surprised," she finally answered. "Where are you from originally? Norway? You don't have an accent." She kept the small talk going to distract herself from the discomfort of holding the awkward position. At least, that's what she told herself. It had nothing to do with him touching her. Not at all.

"I'm from Alaska, actually, though my dad is of mostly Norwegian descent. Mom is American and a little bit Inuit." He paused to focus on her injuries, but spoke again a moment later. "What about you? California girl?"

"Nah. Seattle."

She could've gone into more detail, but she was used to playing her cards very close to her vest. Being mer meant being secretive. Also, her back hurt like a son of a bitch, so she really wasn't up to holding a detailed conversation.

"This hurts a lot more than you're letting on, doesn't it?" he asked softly, surprising her. "I'm almost done, but let's reposition you. I think if you sit up, it won't hurt as bad."

She hadn't sat up yet. Not on her own. The only near-sitting-up position she'd achieved had been courtesy of the electronic bed that allowed her to raise and lower her feet and head.

"Are you sure that's wise?" she asked, not

totally embracing the idea.

Her abdomen was still a mess. The muscles there didn't really want to work right now, not with all the stitches, scabs, nascent scars and bruising.

"I think we should at least try it. Come on, lean on me." He moved slightly, letting her slide onto her back, then guided her arms up to his shoulders so that she was almost hugging him. His hands supported her at the sides of her waist—the only spots on her midsection that hadn't been cut up by the creature's jaws. "I'm going to put my hand between your shoulder blades and lift you upright. Just hang on to my shoulders."

Without giving her much more warning than that, he lifted her up into a sitting position. She wasn't actually supporting herself. She was more or less draped over him, her head resting against his hard shoulder as she gasped, catching her breath.

Holy shit! That had hurt. But as the pain faded to background, she realized he'd been right. Having the weight off her back felt good.

"Okay?" he asked quietly.

"Yeah, it's better this way, but I can't support myself yet." She hated admitting to weakness, but it was very obvious. If she could've held her own weight, she wouldn't be hugging him. Though...she had to admit, hugging him was a very nice place to be.

"That's all right. It'll come in time."

She was very aware of the thin fabric separating them. Her hospital gown gaped open in the back, and he had his arms around her waist so he could continue working on her wounds. He'd already cleaned and treated them. Now, he was just bandaging her up again.

"Even just sitting up in an easy chair takes a bit of the weight off your back and might help speed the healing," he said, his deep voice so much closer now that she was leaning against him. "As your energy comes back, so will your healing ability. I've seen it before. You're on the mend, Sirena."

"It doesn't feel like it," she groused. "I hate this." And she hated the little hitch in her voice that almost sounded like tears.

His touch changed then. He finished with her wounds, and one of his strong, capable hands went to the back of her head, stroking her hair. He was soothing her. She'd heard land shifters liked the reassurance of touch, and she hadn't really understood it...until this very moment.

"It'll be okay. I promise." His murmured words and soft touches helped, in some indefinable way, to make her feel better. Stronger.

"If it's all right with you, I'd like to ask Gus, our shaman, to come and take a look at you. He was here right after we patched you up, but you wouldn't remember. You were out cold."

"What does a shaman do, exactly?" Mer didn't have shamans. They had power places deep in the oceans, sacred to Poseidon.

"Well, Gus can give me an evaluation of your magical levels. The leviathan and its smaller friends—as near as we can figure—drain shifter magic. It had its hooks in your friend, Grace, not too long ago, and I'd like to make sure there isn't some residual link between one of those monsters and you. Gus checked a few days ago, like I said, but I'd like him to check again. Just to be sure."

"So he's a magic user? Is he human?"

"Gus? No. He's a spirit bear." Sven said the words like they were a title she should recognize, then shrugged. "It's a Native thing. He helps out on the reservation to the south and also serves our community. He

22

lives between the two in a lot of different ways."

"He's an Indian?" The image was coming a bit clearer in her mind, but she'd never met an Indian shaman before.

"Yeah. Part, at least," Sven answered.

"And a shifter?" She was still skeptical.

"Yep. The only one like him in our community. He's a good man."

"All right." She didn't want to second guess the doctor.

He'd been so good to her—and her people. All the bears had been nothing but helpful. It was her own damned fault she was feeling so suspicious of everything and angry with the world for being injured.

"Good. Now, let's see if we can sit up the bed as far as it'll go. Then, I'll get the easy chair in here and set it up for when you're ready." Neither of them moved. She felt too good, being held by him. "Uh…you'll have to let me go, though, honey."

"Oh!" She withdrew her hands from around his shoulders. "Sorry. Guess I got too comfortable there for a minute."

Could she be any more inane? Sirena tried to hide her embarrassment with humor, but it wasn't that convincing. She'd just felt better than she had in days, and it was all due to the nearness of this...this...annoying Norwegian-American-Inuit polar bear who made her want things she just couldn't have. Things she didn't believe in anymore.

Sven reached past her to hit the control that raised the bed. The motion brought their torsos in contact again, and she was ultra-aware of the hardness of his chest against her breasts—bare under the thin hospital gown. She felt the bed moving under her as he gently lowered her.

She didn't have far to go. He'd raised the head of the bed all the way. It wasn't quite sitting up, but it was higher than she'd pushed the bed until now.

When he pulled back, she was sorry to lose him. He was so big and warm. Comforting in a way she hadn't been comforted since she was a small child. He felt so safe. As if he'd never let anything hurt her ever again.

After the shock she'd had—fighting a being not of this world, and losing—she had thought she'd never feel safe again. She'd been wrong. Sven represented safety to her right now. Hopefully, in time, she'd find her footing again and regain the confidence she'd lost in that encounter with the creature straight from hell.

She wouldn't rest easy until that damned thing was banished to the farthest realm.

"How does that feel?"

For a moment, she didn't know what he was referring to. She'd been lost in horrible memories and anger.

The bed. Her back. He'd been asking about the position he'd put her in with the head of the bed up as far as it would go.

"It's okay. Thanks." She tried to refocus her mind, but just that little exertion had knocked her out. Her energy levels were at an all-time low.

"I'm going to ask Gus to come up here and check on you," Sven said as he headed for the door. "Sit tight."

"I'm not going anywhere," she mumbled as he left, feeling what little energy she had left desert her as she fell into a light doze that must have lasted more than an hour.

The next thing she knew, a stranger was knocking politely on the partially open door to her room. His skin had a beautiful Native American tone to it, his features sharp and his eyes somewhat mystical.

"You must be the shaman," she said,

opening her eyes fully and blinking a few times, trying to wake up.

"Guilty as charged, ma'am. I'm Gus. How are you feeling?"

"Like a sea monster's chew toy," she grumbled. To her satisfaction, Gus chuckled.

"If you don't mind my saying, you look a lot better than you did the last time I saw you." He moved into the room, and Sven was right behind him, watching all but saying nothing. "Of course, you were unconscious then, and bleeding a lot. Your magic was drained in a way I've never encountered before."

"Is it any better now? Can you tell just from looking at me?"

She almost didn't want to believe in the shaman's power. It was disconcerting to know how close to death she had been and exactly what the evil creature had been doing to her—absorbing her magic, feeding on her energy.

"As Sven must've already told you, you're doing a lot better. It'll still take some time for you to regain what was lost, but I have high hopes that you'll be back in fighting form in a matter of weeks."

"Weeks?" That sounded uber-depressing

to Sirena. As a powerful mer creature, she was used to healing the very worst wounds in days—not weeks.

Gus chuckled again. It was a warm sound, but as handsome as the shaman was, he didn't do it for her like the doc. Sven's slightest smile sent shivers down her spine and tingles to her lady parts. Gus, while attractive, didn't have quite the same effect. Not by a long shot.

"Don't knock it. Weeks is good, considering how far gone you were just a few days ago. And if your spirit is as strong as I suspect, it could be a little sooner." Gus pulled over the guest chair and sat at her bedside. "Now, if you'll allow me, I can do a small ceremony that might help. A blessing, if you will, though I'm pretty sure the way you practice your faith underwater is a little different than what we do on land. What do you say?"

"You serve the Goddess?" Sirena wasn't sure. Most land shifters served the Goddess, but didn't Native Americans have different beliefs?

Gus nodded. "The Mother of All. The Great Spirit. The divine power of the universe is known by many names. All

27

creatures of Light serve that spirit, and I am but one more humble servant."

That sounded kind of beautiful. Poetic, even.

"All right then," she agreed softly, closing her eyes. She was still feeling wrung out from the doctor's earlier ministrations.

The shaman began to chant. Low at first, the masculine sounds thrummed through her, leaving energy in their wake. Pure energy. Goddess-blessed and good.

It gave her a little boost, though she was still very weak. It was enough, though, to ease some of the constant pain and allow her to drift into the first really deep, natural sleep she'd experienced since the attack.

CHAPTER THREE

Gus walked out of Sirena's room looking a bit pale, but moving all right, if Sven was any judge. He'd seen the shaman give of his own energies before and knew the signs.

"How bad is it?" Sven guided Gus to a chair in the waiting room, well away from Sirena's partially open door.

"Me or her?" Gus asked with a crooked smile as he collapsed into the chair.

"Both?" Sven stood over his friend, trying to assess his overall health without being too obvious about it.

"I'll be fine in a minute. She's going to take a bit longer. You were right about something feeding off her magical energy. It took her down to almost nothing. In fact, like I told you when I first saw her, I'm amazed she survived at all. Never mind the physical injuries. The damage to her spirit was substantial. But she's strong. She's slowly beginning to bounce back." Gus took a deep breath and shut his eyes for a moment.

Sven took that opportunity to reach into the small refrigerator he kept in his office. He brought a sandwich he'd been saving for a snack over to Gus and handed it to him. The shaman took it gratefully and wolfed it down. When you used up a lot of energy, sometimes food helped.

"I don't think she's linked to the creature any longer," Gus said, pausing in between bites. "As far as I can tell, she got away clean, though her energy is so low, it's hard to really tell. I guess the creature thought it had drained her and had no further use for her. It would cost it a bit of its own energy to maintain an open pathway. I think it opted to just let her go, thinking she was already dead. Or would be soon. Only, your Sirena is more of a fighter than it thought."

"So there's no residual connection?" That was vital. Sven could watch over her physical injuries as they healed, but if the leviathan's friend still had its hooks in her somehow...*that* he couldn't handle on his own.

"From what I can see, no. Her energy reserves are still very low and hard to discern, but she's beginning to bounce back, magically speaking, and I can't see any obvious drains on that. It's just going to take time." Gus stood, rolled up the sandwich wrapper and chucked it in the trash. He then stepped over to the water cooler and drank several cups of the spring water Sven kept on hand. Gus was looking better, Sven was pleased to see. "I'll help in any way I can, but I think the best thing for her right now is just what you're doing—letting her rest and rebuild her strength gradually."

Sven held out his hand to his friend. "Thanks, Gus. I'm grateful for you coming over here to check on her."

They shook hands, and Gus nodded and smiled faintly. "Glad to be of help. Will you still be able to do clinic hours on the reservation tomorrow?"

Gus was the main go-between with the Indian reservation that bordered Grizzly Cove to the south. He cared greatly for the people there, many of whom didn't have access to regular medical care or the usual amenities of modern everyday life.

"I'll be there. Wouldn't miss it," Sven replied. "As long as there aren't any emergencies."

"Of course." Gus backed away and headed for the door. "I'll see you tomorrow then."

As Gus left, Sven heard a bit of commotion from Sirena's room. He went back to check on her and found her trying to sit up on the edge of the bed. She'd thrown her legs over the side and was struggling, pulling at the sheets, trying to lever herself upright. At a glance, it looked like she was winning the battle, but Sven rushed to her side anyway, not wanting her to reopen any of her wounds in the fight.

"Hey, sweetheart, what do you think you're doing?" Sven asked her in what was meant to be a cajoling tone but came out a bit accusatory despite his best efforts. He wasn't the best with patients. Something about being a bear made him impatient when dealing with non-shifters or shifters who were slow to heal.

"I'm trying to get up and go to the

bathroom. I'm sick of needing help to do the simplest things." She sounded angry as she grabbed onto his forearms. He held her by the shoulders, steadying her.

"Hang on there, honey. I'm not sure—"

"Well, I am!" She cut off his words, showing a bit of temper. "I'm sick of lying in bed. I'm sick of not being able to even go pee without help. I'm sick of being helpless."

Sirena cringed when her voice broke on that last bit. She was sick of being so weak, both physically and mentally. And now, the bear doc was just looking at her. She had to lower her eyes, ashamed of her outburst and her condition.

The next thing she knew, she was being lifted into the air, Sven's strong arms supporting her, one at her back and one under the bend of her knees. He carried her to the attached bathroom. It wasn't a big room, but there was just enough room for him to set her on her feet in front of the toilet.

There were handholds everywhere, designed especially for people who were unsteady or impaired to be able to hang on to something. Sirena made use of the steel bars that ran on either side of the toilet— one on the wall and one on the side of the vanity that held the sink.

"Can you manage from here?" Sven asked in a gentle tone. Sirena nodded. "Yank on this cord when you're ready to go back, and I'll come get you. Or if you get into trouble. I'll be just outside."

He turned to go, and she felt tears in her eyes. "Doc?" she heard herself say. He turned to look back at her, and she gave him a shaky smile. "Thanks."

"I know it's hard to be laid up," was all he said as he walked out and closed the door. It wasn't locked, but she knew he wouldn't come charging in until she signaled—or if she took too long and he became concerned.

With that in mind, she slid the hospital gown out of the way and sat, grateful for the handholds and the easy access of the simple covering. Thinking about the gown, she realized that Sven had probably seen her naked. He'd sewn her up, after all. But since she'd regained consciousness, he'd always shown her the utmost respect and allowed for her modesty.

He didn't have to. Shifters were used to nakedness, though mer were a bit different than land-based shifters. When she wore her scales, they effectively hid most of her physical attributes. They were like armor, of a sort. A covering that made one mer look very much like another.

It was when they shifted to skin that the differences became more obvious. Mer didn't shift often. Only when going from land to water and vice versa, which was something they didn't do all that often, as a general rule. Some mer would live ashore half the year and in the ocean the other half. Many families with children would spend the school year on land and summer in the sea.

Land shifters probably changed form all the time. Not so with mer. That's why mer were a little more modest and tended to cover up their human skin rather quickly, feeling somewhat naked without the armor of their scales. She wondered what it was like for bears. Did they feel naked in human form, without their fur?

Sirena finished up in the lavatory, pulling herself upright with the aid of the rails, then spent a few minutes washing her hands, then using the new toothbrush and toothpaste she found on the vanity to brush her teeth. She found a comb as well and tried to do something with her hair.

What she really needed was a shower, but her strength was already beginning to ebb. She'd kept herself upright by force of will alone, but even that was deserting her. Quickly, she pulled the cord and noticed a light go on above the door. There was a light on the outside too, she knew.

A few seconds later, Sven opened the door and simply swept her up into his arms as if she weighed nothing at all. He carried her to the bed, which she noticed had been made with fresh sheets while she'd been in the bathroom. Since there was nobody else in the building, Sven must've done it.

He laid her down on the clean white sheet and pulled a matching cover over her, up to her waist. She felt so good to have gotten out of bed and cleaned up a bit.

"Thank you, Sven. I'm wiped out now, but it was well worth it. And thanks for making the bed."

"All part of the service, ma'am. Sorry I ran out of chocolates for your pillow." He winked at her as he stepped back. "I did refresh your water, though." He nodded toward the bedside table that held not just one, but three full pitchers of ice water.

He was learning. She smiled back at him. "We mer do need our water. Thanks for that as well, doctor."

"A minute ago, you called me Sven. Now, I'm back to *doctor*?" She saw a teasing light in his eyes that dared her to play with him. Were polar bears playful?

Sirena shrugged, trying to keep it light. Using his given name had been a slip. She hadn't meant to become so familiar with the man so quickly. There was an undercurrent of attraction that made her want to step over all sorts of bounds with the sexy bear shifter, but she was mer. She had to remember where her true loyalties should lie—with her own kind.

"Sorry."

The silence dragged a bit. She couldn't meet his gaze but knew he was looking at her. What was he thinking? She had no idea, and, she reminded herself sternly, she really shouldn't care. He was a landlubber. She'd tried that before—getting involved with a man on land—but it had never worked out, and she was too old to break her own heart again.

"Well...uh..." he began, but was halted from saying anything else by the arrival of

Beth, a fellow mer and one of Sirena's hunting party.

Beth and some of the other girls had been sitting with Sirena off and on while she was laid up. Before today, she had been aware of them but unable to really spend much time talking. She'd been sleeping mostly. Today, however, she felt a bit better—especially since the shaman's visit—and she wanted to catch up on what was going on outside while she was stuck in here.

Sirena looked up at Sven then, realizing he was still standing near the door. He looked at Beth, then back at Sirena, seeming a little lost. What that might indicate, she had no idea. And she wasn't interested. Really. Not at all.

"I'll leave you two alone. I'm going to run out and pick up dinner if that's all right with you. Want anything special, Sirena?" Sven asked.

"Anything but fish. Maybe roast beef? Or turkey?" she suggested.

"Coming right up. I'll be back in a bit. If you need me before then, just call the bakery. Number's in the book by the phone." He gestured to the bedside table, and she saw the small telephone directory—

a single page—lying under the phone. He'd thought of just about everything to make her stay comfortable. Now that she was more awake, she'd be taking better advantage of it.

"Thanks, doc," she told him, watching after him when he nodded and turned to walk away.

Beth poured a glass of water and handed it to her.

"He's okay, for a bear, I guess," was Beth's somewhat surprising comment. Sirena looked at her friend.

"He saved my life. That makes him okay in my book," Sirena said quietly, watching Beth closely. Sirena had never really been sure of Beth. She could be very cutting at times and was a bit of a loner—even for a mer, which was saying something.

"Technically, it was Jetty's mate, Drew, who saved your life. All of our lives, really," Beth pointed out. "He's the nicest of the bears I've met so far, but all he sees is Jetty, so I don't really know him that well. He seems devoted to her, which counts in his favor to my mind."

So clinical. Beth didn't really show emotion. The term *cold fish* fit her to a T, unfortunately.

"That's the way it's supposed to be with mates. They only see each other and are devoted for life. It's kind of beautiful, actually." Sirena sipped her water, thinking about how her parents still looked at each other all these years later. They were true mates.

"If you say so." Beth shrugged as if it didn't really matter, and Sirena thought that was really, really sad. Beth didn't even seem to care if she ever found love like that of a true mate. What was wrong with the woman?

CHAPTER FOUR

If Sirena could find a male to love her, who she could love in return, she'd count herself Goddess blessed. She wanted love in her life. She wanted a true mate most of all, even if she presented an austere front to the world. She was a warrior. She had to be tough on the outside, but that didn't mean she didn't have a tender female heart on the inside.

A guy like the doctor would be perfect, if he were mer. Or even human. Mer often mated with humans and stayed on land during the lifespan of their human partner. There were few male mer, and most of those could have their pick of the females. Of course, there had to be that spark of mating hunger that struck them both to make the mating stick. A blessing from Poseidon, some called it.

Two of Sirena's friends and hunting party subordinates had recently mated with bear shifters, and they claimed to be true mates, but Sirena wasn't completely certain. It *looked* like both Grace and Jetty had found true mates, but how could Sirena be sure?

Mating with different species of magical folk was frowned upon in the pod. Mate with mer or mortal, was the saying. Any Others would only bring difficulties to the pod that they didn't want to deal with. Of course, now that the entire pod was sheltering in Grizzly Cove, maybe the increased interaction with land shifters would bring about new understanding.

Jetty and Grace's choices to mate with bears hadn't gone down well with the pod, but they were adjusting. Jetty's mate's actions in fighting the leviathan and protecting the mer while they raced to safety in the cove had gained the bears new respect. Likewise, the Alpha bear's mate had started to gain popularity once it was discovered she was the witch—she called herself a *strega*, which was some kind of hereditary Italian mage designation—who had cast permanent wards around the town and the waters of the cove itself.

That kind of magic was rare, and that she'd used it for such a pure purpose left the pod in little doubt of her innate goodness. Though the mer usually had little to do with magic users of any kind, there seemed to be a general feeling of acceptance of the *strega* and her sister.

"Are you up to visitors?" a new female voice came from the doorway.

Sirena looked up to see who had come, and as if she had conjured them by thinking of them, there stood Urse and Mellie, the two *strega*. It must be them. Their magic tingled along Sirena's senses. Both were smiling and holding small parcels in their hands.

"We thought you might be getting bored sitting in here all day, and since we own the bookstore in town, we brought along some reading material you might like," the younger one, Mellie, explained, holding up the stack of paperbacks in her hands.

"You read my mind," Sirena said, motioning for them to come in. Beth sat in the room's only chair, so the sisters stood at the side of the bed. "I haven't read a book in at least a year. They don't do so well underwater."

The sisters laughed at Sirena's little joke, as she'd intended. She wanted to know more about these women, and this seemed to be a good opportunity.

"I hope you don't mind us barging in like this," the older sister said. "I'm Urse, and this is my sister, Mellie. We ran into Sven in the café, and he asked us to bring some books by for you. He said you might be up to some reading in the next few days as you heal."

"It was very kind of you to come by," Sirena answered. "I'm Sirena, as you probably know, and this is Beth. Have you already met?"

The three women shook their heads, and Sirena silently encouraged Beth to be cordial to the two magical sisters. After all, they had come bearing gifts.

They spent a few minutes looking at the selection of books the sisters had brought, and Sirena picked out three paperbacks that looked interesting. The sisters declined payment of any kind, insisting that they were get-well presents and inviting Sirena to come visit their bookshop when she was back on her feet.

It was a good thing they didn't want payment, Sirena reflected, because she didn't have access to any of her belongings. She'd come here wearing her scales, and little else. It would take some time and a few phone calls—maybe some computer time too—to procure things like her identification, credit cards and cash. It could be managed, but not easily from a hospital bed.

"I have to say, your people are really moving fast in bringing the town into the twenty-first century," Mellie said conversationally. "There are already two more ATMs in town, and a branch of a major bank is opening in the next week. I had no idea mer were so industrious. Or that they even existed at all, really. And we finally got a clothing store that sells women's fashions and not just tourist T-shirts and shorts."

"Although, they're actually stocking T-shirts that say Grizzly Cove on them now, which is something the town council didn't allow before. I think, with the sudden increase in population, they're realizing they're going to have to accept that there will be more tourists coming through and more contact with the human world," Urse added. "I know John always thought a tourist trade would help support the running of the town eventually, but events have happened a bit faster than he expected. The arrival of your people has helped hasten putting our town on the map, so to speak, and increased contacts with the outside world. As soon as the weather brightens and we open a few more businesses on Main Street, I think we're going to see a big increase in human traffic."

"You sound as if you're looking forward to it," Sirena observed, trying to figure the witch out.

Urse smiled. "You know, I am. I've enjoyed the isolation here since we moved in, but I think the town is just about ready for the next step in its evolution. More people will mean that more of the men here might have a chance at finding the happiness John and I have found. These are good men, and they deserve a shot at happy futures."

Sirena was impressed by the honesty she heard in Urse's voice.

"That's what I want for my own people,

as well," Sirena told the other woman. "I know Grace and Jetty don't want me to worry, but I can't help but wonder, until I can see things for myself."

Urse seemed to consider her words, then slowly nodded. "Well, I'm confident that once you're on your feet again, you'll find your friends are very happy with their mates. And your folk have been changing the face of Grizzly Cove almost overnight." Urse cracked a smile. "It's almost more than my poor John can take. For so long, they struggled to get this sleepy little town off to a good start, and now, suddenly, things are changing faster than the bears ever expected. I think it'll all work out for the best in the end, but it's been amusing to watch the mer move in and pretty much take over. You guys are like industrious little gnomes, building things seemingly overnight."

"Gnomes?" Beth sounded outraged, and Sirena had to laugh.

"The cute ones," Urse assured Beth in a teasing tone. "Little red hats, can-do attitude, jolly outlook on life."

"You haven't met a lot of mer, have you?" Sirena countered, amused by the witch's description.

"Not until recently," Urse admitted. "You don't see it, but when I think about how quiet the town was just last week and how it is today… Your people have had a heck of an influence in a very short time."

"For the good, I hope," Sirena said.

"Mostly, I think," Urse agreed. "But I'll let you know once I meet a few more mer and see what happens to the town in the end."

"Generally, we try to leave a place better than we found it," Sirena tried to reassure the witch. "Part of our duties when we're in the ocean is to help Mother Nature clean it up. We do the same on land, for the most part, when we spend time ashore."

Urse nodded. "Good to know. Hopefully, that'll reassure John. Between you and me, I think he's a little afraid of your leader, Nansee. He told me he thinks she might have a shark fin when she shifts."

Sirena burst out laughing. Beth just frowned.

Just then, they all turned when Sven appeared at the open door, a brown shopping bag in his hands. Delicious aromas were wafting from inside the bag. It smelled as if dinner had arrived.

"I guess that's our cue to leave," Mellie said, smiling. "Just call the shop if you want any other books, okay? We're just down the street, and I can run them up to you, no problem."

"That's really sweet of you," Sirena said, meaning it. The two witches were much less scary than she'd imagined they'd be. "Thanks."

"No problem. Great meeting you. Feel better soon!"

Mellie bounced out of the room, giving Sven a grin on her way out. Her older sister was a little more sedate, but she reiterated the offer to bring by more reading material, then said goodbye. All in all, Sirena had formed a favorable opinion of the two women during their visit, which surprised her. She'd never been overly fond of magic workers. Not that she'd had a lot of exposure to any, though she had crossed paths with a few, here and there, when she'd lived on land.

Mostly, she just gave mages a wide berth, and they did the same. These two sisters though... They were really nice. Much nicer than she'd expected given her previous experience with standoffish mages doing all they could to either intimidate her or go far out of their way to stay clear of her.

Beth looked from Sven to Sirena and apparently decided to leave as well. She said a quiet goodbye to Sirena and slipped out while the doctor set up the rolling table that adjusted to fit over her bed.

When he looked up from his task, he gave her a smile. "Looks like I still know how to clear a room. All the girls run off when I show up."

"I don't think it has anything to do with you, Doc. It's more like they're letting the invalid eat in peace. I'm just as glad not to have an audience. I'm weak as a kitten right now, and it doesn't sit well with me." She shifted position in the bed, trying to find a more comfortable angle for her back.

Sven stopped and looked at her. "It's not easy for a strong person to be laid low by injury. I see it often enough in my profession, but this is only a temporary setback for you."

"It doesn't feel temporary."

CHAPTER FIVE

He could've leaned over and kissed her then, but she seemed in no mood to be pawed by a polar bear. She just looked so forlorn, he wanted to wrap her up in a comforting bear hug, but this was one prickly fish, and he didn't want to do anything to antagonize her right now. He'd only just put her back together. He didn't need her tearing him—or herself—apart because he got too aggressive too soon.

Or at all.

Sven didn't understand why, but this mermaid called to his bear half more than any other female he'd ever encountered. The bear wanted to bask in her scent and roll onto its back at her feet in surrender.

As a rule, his bear was a brawler, not a creature that had ever even considered surrendering to anyone or anything. Yet... The mermaid brought out all sorts of instincts he didn't understand.

Even the human part of him was affected. Sure, like most men, Sven had always been attracted by a pretty face, but there was something deeper in his attraction to Sirena. Something more primal. Animal—even in his human form.

He wanted her. But more than that, he wanted her whole and healthy, and he wanted her to choose him back. Desperately.

"You said turkey or roast beef, so I got both. I thought maybe you wouldn't mind my company for dinner. Thought maybe we could talk a bit. Get to know each other," he ground out as he piled the table between them with food. *Smooth, Sven, real smooth.*

Sirena looked puzzled when he dared to glance up to check her expression. After a beat, she spoke.

"Sure. I'd like the company, but you shouldn't have gone to so much trouble. You brought back enough food for an army."

"Bears eat a lot. I wasn't sure how much the average mer might like, so I figured I'd err on the side of caution. Anything we don't finish tonight, I can put in the fridge, and I can have it for lunch tomorrow. I always try to keep the fridge stocked with a bit extra anyway, in case somebody comes in. Food is part of shifter healing. Helps restore the energy our bodies use when they heal." He finished laying out the sandwiches and utensils, letting her take her pick.

"Mer aren't exactly the same as land-based shifters, but I guess we do eat more than humans, when we have successful hunts. Of course, we can also go for a day or two without eating if we're in a bare patch of ocean." She grabbed the turkey sandwich closest to her first, and he took one of his own. He'd gotten three of each, just in case, plus some treats for dessert.

"Well, bears can go a while without food too, but we certainly don't like it." He took a huge bite of the turkey on rye. The gals at the bakery certainly knew how to make a good sandwich.

"You mean you guys don't hibernate like your wild cousins?" The playful tone in her voice made him look up, and he was struck by the dancing light in her eyes.

"Even my non-shifting polar bear cousins don't really hibernate. That's strictly a brown and black bear thing. Pregnant polar females will den up in the snow and not eat for a few months while they have their cubs, but males, and females who aren't pregnant, just keep moving even in the harshest conditions. Hunting, living. Their metabolic rates drop a bit to help them stay warm, but they don't hibernate. And neither do I." He took another bite of his sandwich. "Not that the idea of sleeping in doesn't appeal to me now and again." He winked at her and was charmed by her answering smile.

"My mistake," she said softly, nibbling on her sandwich in a way that made him wonder what those lush lips would feel like if she used them on his skin.

"How do you like the food?" he asked when the silence had dragged a bit too long.

"My compliments to the chef. This is seriously delish." She popped the last bite of the turkey sandwich into her mouth and reached for the roast beef. "Got any mustard?"

Sven reached for the little jar Tina had included in the bag. It was a fancy spicy brown mustard they had brought in at her mate's urging. Zak wasn't just a black bear, but he was also the finest Cajun chef in town—or in the state, for that matter. His new restaurant was nearing completion. The funding had come from a surprising silent partner—the Master vampire of Seattle, old Hiram Abernathy.

That project had marked a new era of cooperation and a very visible sign of the truce between the vamps and weres in Grizzly Cove and Seattle, which wasn't too far away as the crow flies. Sven wondered what the mer would make of the ties between the bears of Grizzly Cove and Master Hiram.

Deciding to leave the politics to those better suited to deal with such things, he uncapped the mustard jar and handed it over to Sirena along with a plastic knife. Her eyes lit up when she saw the gourmet brand.

"Fancy," she said, slathering her sandwich with the golden goodness. When she'd finished, there wasn't much left in the tiny jar, but that was okay. Tina had sent along another, which Sven was keeping in reserve for now.

For some reason, he was transfixed by

the sight of Sirena biting into the fresh sandwich, her luscious lips surrounding the bread and meat. Mustard oozing.

Sven had never thought the act of eating a sandwich could be sexually stimulating before, but he'd been wrong. Sirena, thank the Goddess, seemed oblivious to the fact that Sven had to squirm in his chair as his jeans suddenly became uncomfortably tight in the crotch area.

Shit. He'd just gotten a hard on from watching her eat. What was *wrong* with him? She was injured. Weak. A patient in his care, for goodness sake!

But she was also the sexiest thing he'd ever seen. Even at less than half strength, she was a force to be reckoned with. Her strength of spirit appealed to his bear side, and his human side. Sirena was a woman who sparked his long-dormant interest in new and exciting ways.

Sven squirmed a bit more in his chair, grateful that the high table was between them. With any luck, she'd never know how inappropriately turned on he'd become by watching her eat dinner.

"So, what do you usually do around here? I know shifters heal notoriously fast, so there probably isn't much call for a doctor most of the time, is there?" Sirena asked between bites.

Her question broke his stupor and shook him back to his senses a bit. "You'd be surprised. Just lately, I've been kept hopping by a certain sea monster and the damage it's been inflicting on my friends and their mates and allies. But even before that, there was enough to keep me busy. While you're right about shifters not really catching diseases or even the common cold very often, we do manage to get banged up now and again." He reached for another sandwich and tried to concentrate on telling her about his work rather than the still-uncomfortable fit of his jeans. "We've had a few construction accidents while we've been building. Broken bones to set. Dislocated shoulders to pop back in. Then, there are the brawls. We had quite a few while figuring out the new hierarchy here in town. It's not natural for so many bears to congregate together in one place. It's been…" How did he describe the series of challenges and fights that had characterized their first months setting up this place without alarming the mermaid? "It's been…interesting times."

"I bet," was her only comment as she focused on her sandwich. That despicable, loathsome, lucky son of a sandwich that had her lips wrapped around it...again. Shit. He was going to bust the zipper on his jeans if she kept doing that. "So you're basically a trauma man, then? You deal with injuries more often than disease?"

"Pretty much all the time. Oh, once in a while someone will get a sniffle, but aside from handing out the occasional pain med, I don't do a lot for the adults. The kids, on the other hand, get into more mischief than I thought they would, though we don't have a lot of cubs in town yet. As far as adults go, our shifter healing does the bulk of the work around here."

"That'll change if you get more humans coming through. They get sick a lot," she observed.

"That's true. And it's something I've been thinking about. We may need to expand these facilities if traffic picks up. Having only one room for overnight patients was a bit shortsighted. We should probably build on and add another room. Maybe two. Just in case. And they could be used for non-medical emergencies too, when someone needs a place to sleep and there's no other option available for whatever reason."

"You *have* been thinking about this. I'm impressed." Thankfully, she finished with the sandwich and seemed to take a break from eating for the moment, sipping at her water instead.

"Well, that's the role I've agreed to play for the town. Doctor and safe port in a storm, so to speak. I never thought I'd be dealing with your folk though, so I'm going to have to brush up on mer, in general. If this situation becomes as permanent as it appears it might, then I'd even consider hiring a mer to work in the clinic, once it's expanded. If this place is going to get bigger and busier, I'll need help."

"Very forward thinking of you," she said, looking at him from under her lashes while she sipped more water. "But what do you mean about permanence exactly?"

"I mean after we defeat the leviathan. If the mer still want to use Grizzly Cove as a base, then some of you might want to build homes here. This could be a good place for your folk to come and go from the water in a protected environment, where you could put down roots on land that would be waiting for you, protected by us and our alliance with your folk, whenever you want to return."

"I hadn't really thought that far ahead," Sirena admitted, though she seemed impressed, rather than skeptical, of the idea.

"Truth be told, I didn't either. It's something John came up with. He's the long-term strategist. He's the one who planned the whole concept of the town, long before he ever told us about it. That's why we made him Alpha. He's always had our best interests at heart, and now, that includes you and your people too."

"I assume he's been discussing all these long-term plans with Nansee, our pod leader?" Sirena asked, one eyebrow raised in a quizzical expression.

"She's staying at his place," Sven told her. "Nell set her up in their guest room. I bet they're plotting and planning over every meal."

Sirena seemed to take in that information as she finished her water. "Do you mind if I tackle another roast beef sandwich?"

"Not at all," he said while inwardly wondering how he was going to get through watching her devour another mustardy creation. He handed over the second little bottle of mustard before she even asked.

When she started eating the second roast beef sandwich, it was all he could do to remain seated. He matched her bite for bite as he ate the last sandwich and tried really hard not to stare at her gorgeous mouth.

And then, the mustard oozed just a bit too far. A little dollop landed on the side of her mouth. It drove him bonkers when she seemed not to notice. The bear inside him sat up as if he'd spotted a succulent treat.

"What?" Sirena seemed to become aware of his rather pointed interest, but he couldn't help himself. He leaned forward, reaching out his hand.

"You've got a little mustard..." He leaned even closer, the table between them the only thing keeping him from licking the condiment off her soft cheek. Instead, he reached out with the index finger of his right hand, touching her gently, wiping away the golden smear.

Her tongue peeped out and touched his finger, and he thought he was going to come in his pants right then and there. Damn.

She held his gaze as she reached farther with her little pink tongue, licking the mustard off his finger, which had stalled, just millimeters from her lips. That was it. He couldn't breathe. Couldn't think of anything but how it would feel if she took his finger—or better yet, his dick—in her mouth.

The image battered at the inside of his skull, but his body was frozen. Polar bear or not, the mermaid had managed to turn him to ice. Hot as hell, but still immobile. She smiled at him as she moved back, leaving him there, holding his finger out like a rube.

"Can't waste any of that delicious mustard," she said, breaking the spell.

Holy shit. This mermaid was potent as hell.

A thought suddenly occurred to him.

"Sirena... You're not part sea siren by any chance, are you?"

She laughed aloud then, her laughter sweet music, like chimes in the still air.

"Why, doctor, I think I'm flattered." Her coy tone made him smile and sit back, finally lowering his hand. "But a girl doesn't reveal that sort of thing on a first date."

That made him sit up again, his back ramrod straight. "Is this a date? If so, I owe you flowers and wine, at the very least."

"How about I take a rain check on that

stuff? I'm more than content at the moment with these yummy sandwiches and spicy mustard." She shrugged. "And as for if it's a date... I'm not really sure. But it is the first time I've shared a meal with a man alone in a few years, so I've had a bit of a dry spell."

"Years?" He couldn't quite believe this beauty wasn't being courted by every male in the ocean.

"I went to sea a few years ago and haven't spent much time on land since. When we're in our mer form, things are a bit...different. And there have always been more females than males among my people."

Sven still couldn't believe it. He'd seen the other mer about town, and Sirena was, by far, the most lovely of them all. Why wasn't she dating? Had someone hurt her? The thought made his inner bear want to growl, but he managed to suppress it. He didn't want to scare her in any way.

He wanted to see her smile again. He wanted to make her happy.

He would work on that long term, but for right now, he had something that might—at least temporarily—put a smile back on her face. He reached for the bakery box he'd set on the side table earlier and opened it up.

"I can't imagine what it's like living beneath the water," he told her gently. "I can't imagine not having access to this sort of thing." He revealed the pastries the Baker sisters had sent along. "The other bears are really partial to the honey buns, but I like these coconut puffs myself." He reached into the box and snagged one, popping it into his mouth. He then offered the box full of sugary goodness to Sirena, gratified to see her try one of the coconut puffs too.

"Mmm. These are amazing," she said around a mouthful of coconutty heaven.

They talked about living on land versus living underwater for a while, nibbling on pastries. He did his best to observe her while not appearing to. She had looked better right after Gus's visit, but the paleness was back, and he could see visible signs of weariness. Sirena had done better today than she had at any time since coming in, but she wasn't healing as quickly as he would like.

When she yawned for the third time, he began cleaning up the remnants of dinner. She needed her rest, and it would be counterproductive for him to stay chatting with her, keeping her awake—no matter how much he wanted to do just that. He was surprised to find himself truly enjoying her company. He didn't want the quiet encounter to end, but she needed sleep, and he needed to study her case notes and try to figure out something else he could do to help her recover.

He stood, taking the trash with him toward the door. "If you need anything during the night, just let me know. I'm sleeping out in the clinic while you're here, so I'll be around."

CHAPTER SIX

Sirena was a really touched that Sven would give up what she was sure was a comfortable bed in his own home to keep an eye on her. She hadn't given much thought to the arrangements before, but he must've been keeping watch over her ever since her arrival.

"I really can't thank you enough for looking after me. I'm sorry to be such a nuisance—"

She would have said more, but he raised one hand forestalling her words.

"It's my job to help those who are in pain, Sirena. Believe it or not, I enjoy it—not that you need my help, of course, but that

I'm able to provide it." He paused by the door, looking away as if in contemplation. "It's my job," he repeated, his voice going lower. "But more than that, it's my calling."

He shook his head as if embarrassed. Perhaps he thought he had said too much, but his words had revealed a much greater depth to the man than she had expected. She was grateful for his candor. It made her feel a little less embarrassed by her situation, by her dependence on him at this moment.

She'd always been a strong woman, standing on her own. She'd never really had such a dire injury before. Being laid up didn't sit well with her, and being beholden to anyone for even her simplest needs made her incredibly uncomfortable.

His words though… His almost unwilling explanation about why he did what he did for a living made her feel somehow better about the situation.

"I'm very grateful to you, Sven," she said softly. The moment felt significant between them. As if they were sharing secrets. "I've never been this weak before, and it's hard to deal with emotionally as well as physically. I appreciate your willingness to help me while I'm down."

"I've been down once or twice myself," he admitted, turning at the door to offer her a lopsided smile. He just looked at her for a moment, their eyes meeting and holding as an understanding energy passed between them. Finally, he looked away, still smiling faintly. "I'll be outside if you need anything. Don't hesitate to ask for help. That's what I'm here for." He walked over the threshold, leaving the door to her room open. "Rest well, Sirena."

"Good night, Sven," she said, confident that, with his sharp shifter senses, he could hear her softly spoken words.

Sven checked on his patient throughout the night, but she didn't wake. She was in a deep sleep that was close to unconsciousness, if he was any judge. She should be getting better now, if there was no power drain on her magic, but she wasn't. Or, if she was, it was incredibly slowly. Even slower than a human.

Sven tried not to worry. He got on the internet—on the special sites hidden deep in the net for shifters—and tried to research her condition, but there was very little information available to him about mer. He supposed they had their own spots on the net where they hid their race's information, but as a polar bear, he had no access. If Sirena didn't start getting better soon, he'd have to approach the pod leader, a rather formidable older woman named Nansee, and see if she'd give him locations and passwords.

In the meantime, he was doing the best he could with the information available, and he did still have one trick up his sleeve. Drew's folks were coming into town within the next day or two. Drew's mother was a powerful priestess who had dragged her son back from the brink of death after he'd been mostly blown up by an improvised explosive device in the desert. She had both magic, the Goddess's blessings and experience with badly injured shifters. Sven would ask her to look at Sirena if she didn't start making better progress.

He hated to doubt Gus's word, but Sirena just wasn't responding the way she should. Gus was a shaman and one of the best people Sven knew, but maybe he'd missed something. Sven couldn't imagine what the spirit bear could have missed, but just maybe he had.

Sirena woke up already feeling tired, which signaled all too clearly how her day was going to go. Downhill.

Sven was altogether too cheerful when he came in to check on her just after she awakened. His smiles were hiding real concern she could feel coming off him in waves. Reassuring he was not, but she felt too lousy to really care.

Everything hurt. Even her hair ached, if that was possible. Now that she was out of the fog of semi- and unconsciousness, she was becoming aware of the real extent and severity of her injuries—and the fact that she didn't seem to be healing.

That should have worried her—and in a small corner of her mind, she was shaking in her mental boots—but in the physical world, she just couldn't work up the energy to feel anxiety. In fact, she wasn't feeling much at all, except frustration.

She wanted out of the infirmary. She wanted to swim and be with her friends. She wanted to hunt and glide through the waters and bask in the sun. She just wanted to be better already.

Was that too much to ask?

"What would you like for lunch?" Sven asked from the doorway. Sirena was confused. Didn't she just have breakfast?

She looked to the window and realized the weak Pacific Northwest sun must have worked its way through the sky faster than she realized. It was directly overhead now, not on the rising side, as she'd thought. She must've missed a few hours, which also was something that should have worried her…if she'd had the energy to worry.

"Not hungry," she mumbled, not really caring.

Sven stepped into the room. She saw him coming and the way his eyebrows drew together in concern. That pissed her off. She couldn't work up energy for worry, but anger didn't seem all that hard.

"Come on, doll. You have to eat something." His voice was coaxing, and he wasn't doing a very good job of hiding that seemingly ever-present concern. It was getting on her nerves.

"Leave me alone." She pulled up the sheet and turned her head away from him.

Strong fingers on her jaw turned her head back, and then, a bright light shone in just one eye while his fingers pried her eyelid open. She swatted at his big hands, but nothing seemed to disrupt his rather rude examination of her eyeballs. He blinded her in one eye, then the other, clucking his tongue against his teeth in a way that set her temper on edge.

"I don't understand it," he muttered, finally stepping back.

Spots floated in front of her eyes as she tried to glare at him. "Will you stop looking at me as some kind of lab rat," she groused.

"Honey—" he began, but she was having none of it.

"Don't you honey me. Leave me alone. I'm tired, and I don't want to talk to you right now." She turned her head away again, her eyes still suffering the illusory spots, though she scrunched them shut against the light.

"I can't, Sirena. I'm your doctor. I need to fix what's wrong with you."

If she'd been feeling sane just then, she might have heard the tone of desperation in his voice, but her understanding had flown along with her worry for self preservation. All she had was anger, and she clung to it.

"Well, thanks a lot, you big, furry, white jackass!" She used the loudest voice she could work up in her weakened condition, surprising even herself with how loud it came out.

"Did you just call me a jackass?" His own temper seemed to have been snagged because his tone rose along with hers. His anger washed over her, fueling...something.

"You bet your bippy I called you a jackass. If the shoe fits, you should wear it!" She wasn't really sure what she was saying by the end there, but she was smoldering with anger. It felt like hers was feeding off his.

And then, he roared.

Right in her face. A good, loud polar bear roar from his human throat.

When he finished, silence reigned for a heartbeat...maybe two. Maybe ten.

She just looked at him, feeling his anger and feeling something...distant...silently egging her on to make him lose control. *What?*

"What in the world is going on here?" an older feminine voice asked from the doorway, breaking the spell.

Sven shook his head as he backed away, his shoulders drooping. He collapsed into the visitor chair, his big frame rattling the poor metal chair in ways that made Sirena think it might give way under him. He rubbed his forehead with one hand, his blue eyes dazed.

"What the hell was that?" he mumbled, clearly shaken.

Sirena didn't feel all that well herself, come to think of it. She shut her eyes and tried to tune out the newcomer, but the woman came over to the bed, ignoring Sven for the moment, and snapped her fingers in front of Sirena's face. Her eyes opened, and the woman started chanting under her breath. Ancient words. Sacred words.

Sirena felt tension. Something was tugging at her. It didn't like the woman or her words of power. The chant grew, and the woman made arcane signs in the air with her hands. So graceful, Sirena thought. So pretty. And powerful.

The tension snapped, and Sirena jumped in the bed, freed from…something.

The woman stopped, sighing as if she'd just used a lot of energy.

"Well." The strange woman put her hands on her hips and turned to survey both Sirena and Sven. "It appears I've arrived just in time. What were you two playing at? You gave that evil thing exactly what it wanted."

She shook her head.

"The sea monster?" Sven asked, regaining some of his energy, though Sirena noticed he didn't move from the chair. "Gus said she was clear of it."

The new lady shook her head. "As much as I respect Gus and his shaman ways, there are some things that require a woman's touch. I'm going to have to talk with John about getting you a permanent priestess for the town. It's clear as day that you need one. Maybe more than one. Especially now."

The woman seemed disapproving and sort of motherly. She wasn't really scolding, more like she was just amazed the men had gotten this far on their own, without a priestess's influence. That was it. The woman must be a priestess.

"You serve the Goddess?" Sirena asked, her voice still weak.

The woman turned her attention back to Sirena and smiled. It was a beautiful smile, like that of Mother Nature smiling on her children. Sirena gasped. Was she seeing the Goddess in the guise of Her servant? Maybe it was just a trick of the light, but...

"Yes, dear. I'm Natalie. I'm Drew's mother. We just got into town to visit with our boy and meet our new daughter-in-law, but I could see from the street that something was wrong in here, so I dropped by here first. I'm glad I did." Natalie put her hand on Sirena's shoulder, and Sirena felt the warmth of Goddess energy that formed a sort of halo around the holy woman.

"I'm glad you did too," Sirena said, smiling at the priestess.

"Make that me three," Sven said, still sitting in the chair. "Can you tell us what just happened, Mrs. Legine? I mean, I can guess, but you're the expert here."

"Call me Natalie, dear," the priestess said to Sven, giving him one of those warm motherly smiles. "If you suspect the creature that harmed her had kept a channel open between itself and our lovely friend here, you're right. I just severed it. The anger you both experienced was something it encouraged so it could feed of both your energies. It likes anger, and it needs all the energy it can get right now because…" She paused. "Well, perhaps that's something I should wait to disclose until I can tell everyone all at once. Sven, would you be a dear and get the town council together? We can meet at the town hall after Andy and I

go drop off our luggage at Drew's. We'll
bring Drew back with us to the hall. I
suspect your patient will be strong enough to
make the short journey there and back by
that time." She smiled at Sirena. "I want her
there because this young lady deserves to
know what I discovered, since she's the
reason I was able to see into the leviathan's
energies. I suspect you'd both be glad for a
change of scene for a little while, no?"

"You're being very mysterious Mrs. L."
Sven stood and seemed to regain his footing,
though his skin was still pale. He went to the
door and shook hands with a big bear of a
man standing watch over them all. He must
be the priestess's mate, the aforementioned
Andy.

It made sense, Sirena thought, that if
Drew had been named for his sire, they
couldn't both use the same nickname. So the
elder must be Andy, while the younger was
Drew.

Sven turned to the woman and gave her a
hug and kiss on the cheek. It was clear he
already knew Drew's parents and was
familiar enough with them both to greet
them as old friends and respected elders.

"Mr. and Mrs. L, this is Sirena of the mer.

She leads the hunting party that your new daughter-in-law was part of before she met Drew." Realizing Sven was making formal introductions, Sirena tried to raise her hand for a polite shake, but the priestess waved her off.

"Conserve your strength, Sirena. You've been through a lot." Mrs. Legine fluffed the pillows behind Sirena's head, helping her find a more comfortable position, her motherly actions making Sirena feel warm and safe. "Rest now. We'll be back in a couple of hours, and we're going to have to have a very serious discussion with the boys. You shouldn't have any more trouble from the creature, but if you feel the slightest discomfort, tell Sven, and I'll be back on the double, okay?"

"Yes, ma'am. Thank you for…" Sirena trailed off between one word and the next, out of steam. She was vaguely aware of Sven walking out the door with the two older bear shifters, and then, it was lights out. She was asleep and truly on the mend.

When Sirena woke, it felt like only moments had passed, but she heard the rumble of Sven's voice out in the clinic beyond her open door. The low tones reminded her of his roar, and she felt a little shiver of excitement. That roar had been sexy.

Surprised by her own response, Sirena thought about it, realizing she was finally thinking clearly for the first time since getting chewed up by the leviathan's minion. A fog had truly lifted from her with Mrs. Legine's intervention. Sirena would have to thank the older woman more formally when she saw her again.

But the doctor captured Sirena's attention again as she heard him hang up the phone and walk around out in the clinic. He was a big man, but he moved almost silently without even trying. Bear tactics, she thought. They were silent hunters in the woods, or so she'd heard. Although, Sven was a polar bear, so he probably hunted on snow and ice.

She'd seen wild polar bears hunting seals from the ice sheets up north on occasion. She'd always given the white bears a wide berth, but had enjoyed watching them. They were so sparkly and huge. Massively muscled and both patient and wild in a way that spoke to the wildness in her own soul. And the little ones were absolutely adorable. So fluffy and cute while they were babies and toddlers.

Sven though... He was a mature male in all his glory, and even in his human form, he retained some of the fearsome might of his animal half. He was stunning, in his way. Magnetic and magical in a way she'd never encountered in a man before.

Tall, of course, built like a linebacker. His eyes sparkled like morning light through clear ice, the blue of the purest water and the cloudless sky. His hair was golden, like the first rays of dawn, and his smile... Well, it was enough to melt her into a little pile of goo.

But when he spoke to her, all bets were off. The timbre of his deep voice went right through her, vibrating up and down her spine, making her tingle all over.

Sirena threw off the covers and decided it was time to test her legs. She felt so much better than she had since being injured. It felt like her mer magic was rebuilding—and helping her rebuild her strength and her body at the same time. She wasn't one-hundred percent just yet, but she felt like the goal was in sight.

First, she'd stand on her own, make it to

the bathroom on her own two legs, then she'd plan out the rest of her day.

CHAPTER SEVEN

As it turned out, Sirena not only made it into the bathroom by herself, but she felt good enough to take advantage of the tiled shower with its built-in bench seat while she was there. She washed her hair with the herbal-smelling shampoo that had a delicate scent—probably because shifter noses were very sensitive.

Her skin soaked in the water, her energy renewing as the moisture bathed her pores in its cleanliness. The bears were fussy about their water, and she was glad of it. This fresh water was purer than anything she could get from municipal water systems when she lived on land. There were no harsh chemicals polluting this water. It was rich with minerals and clear of man-made irritants.

"Sirena?" Sven's voice came to her from just outside the bathroom door. She had closed it, but not locked it.

"I'm just washing up," she called back, glad to feel her strength returning as the cobwebs that had wrapped her mind were washed away.

"If you need help, just let me know," he replied, and she could hear the concern in his voice.

"I need something clean to wear," she told him, realizing that the best way to prove to him that she was finally on the mend was to show him.

"I'll find you something and be right back," he promised. She didn't hear him leave. The water was whooshing over her, and she was enjoying it too much.

A few minutes later, he was back. "I've got some clothes for you. Can I reach in and leave them on the countertop?"

"Yeah, that's okay. I'm still in the shower," she called back, making sure the filmy curtain was closed all the way.

Rationally, she knew he must've seen her body while he was sewing her up, but now that she was awake and feeling more herself, she was shy. He'd always treated her with the utmost respect, and he'd established a sort of precedent by never exposing more of her skin than he needed to in order to change her bandages. Which reminded her…

"I took off the bandages," she said, having heard the door open. "The worst of the cuts look like they've sealed now."

"I can check them, to be sure, when you come out of there," he replied. She thought his voice sounded odd over the swish of the water, but she couldn't be sure.

Sweet mother in heaven, what was she doing to him? Sven tried to get control over himself as he placed the sweatpants and T-shirt on the small countertop beside the sink. Somehow, just knowing she was only feet away, naked, water slicking her soft skin…

Sven adjusted his stance as his jeans suddenly became too tight in a very sensitive area.

"That would be good," she said, her voice coming to him over the sound of the water.

What had they been talking about again? Oh, yeah. Him checking her injuries. Sven frowned. The wounds to her torso had been in rough shape just a few hours ago. He would insist on checking them once she was out of the shower and dressed again. She could just lift the soft sweatshirt and maybe lower the waistband of the pants...

And there he went again. His mind went off on an erotic journey once more, picturing her baring herself to him with a smile of welcome on her face instead of the stoic expressions he'd gotten up 'til now. Or worse, the grimaces of pain she couldn't hide. Sometimes, being a doctor really put a crimp in his love life.

"Clothes are on the countertop. I'll be outside if you need help." He made himself retract his arm and close the door. He wanted more than anything to go in and join her under the shower. Maybe take her in his arms while he ran his fingers over her body. He wanted to be certain she was better, but he had to make himself do it in a way that wouldn't scare her.

The more he'd been around Sirena these past days, the more he realized she was special. Something about her called to him. And to his beast. The bear wanted to sniff her salty scent whenever she was near. She smelled of the sea and of the water. Kelp and delicacies of the ocean that the bear craved.

Polar bears liked the water and the cold. The weather down here in Washington State was a bit mild for his other half, but Sven wouldn't move away from his buddies. After all they'd been through together, the men of his old unit were more like his family than any blood relation he might still claim up in the north. He would stay here, where it was a bit too warm for his polar bear half in the summer, but among the men he thought of as brothers.

Besides, the town needed him. His skills as a doctor had been called upon all too often in recent weeks. While evil stalked his friends and their town, he wouldn't leave. Not even for a quick vacation in the snow. No way, no how.

This leviathan situation was taking its toll on the town and its people. Sven felt responsible for them all, in a way. Not quite like John's Alpha protectiveness, but in a way, the health and wellbeing of the town rested on Sven's shoulders insofar as if anyone got seriously hurt, he was the one best suited to patching them up and making sure nobody died.

While most of his old unit had basic first-aid training, and a few had more advanced skills, Sven was the only credentialed M.D. who could handle the really tough cases. He'd reattached fingers and even a limb or two in his time in the desert with his unit. He could handle major surgery and the few illnesses that sometimes plagued shifters. It took a helluva contagion to bring down a shifter, but Sven knew how to deal with such things where the other guys might not.

Sven heard the click of the doorknob and spun to watch it turn. Then, the door opened, and a waft of steam hit his nose, engulfing him in momentary warmth and the scent of herbal shampoo and woman. Mmm. The bear liked the combination. So did the man.

Sirena smiled at him, and his heart nearly stopped for a moment. She looked so happy. And fit. And the dark circles that had been under her pretty eyes from almost the moment he'd first encountered her were no more.

"You look really good," he said, not realizing the thoughts in his brain were spilling out of his mouth until he heard himself speak.

"I feel really good," she agreed, thankfully not thinking him weird. "The water felt so good, and my energy is starting to return a lot quicker. I think you'd probably better take these stitches out, though, before they get stuck."

She lifted the side of her baggy sweatshirt as she moved toward him and showed him a stretch of creamy skin that made his mouth go dry. Then, he saw his handiwork, and all the lascivious thoughts that had fogged his brain fled. He'd put in quite a few stitches on that particularly nasty wound on her side, and she was right. She was starting to heal like the shifter she was, and those little bits of thread would have to go sooner rather than later.

"I'll get the tray with my tools." He headed out of the room, his mind already on the task in front of him.

When he returned, he found her waiting for him, sitting on the side of the bed, her bare feet dangling over the side. He should have at least found a pair of socks for her.

"I'll get you something to put on your feet as soon as we have those stitches out, all right?" He approached, all business as he tried to work out the best way to approach her now that she was mobile. "Would you lie down on your side for me?"

She complied, moving much easier now that she was on the mend. It did his heart good to see her responding the way any of his shifter comrades would have from such wounds. The lack of progress before Mrs. Legine's intervention was now glaringly obvious. He could only send his thanks heavenward to the Mother of All that Mrs. Legine had arrived when she had.

Come to think of it, since Drew's mother was a priestess, it very well could have been divine intervention that sent her here at the exact moment she was needed. Sven had seen stranger things in his time. He wouldn't be surprised at all if the Goddess hadn't been watching over Her servants just the tiniest bit.

Sirena got in position, and Sven dragged a chair over to her bedside. He laid his tools out on the edge of the bed next to her hip. He'd brought scissors, tweezers, topical disinfectant and gauze with him in a metal dish. He emptied the dish of the supplies and would use it to catch the used sutures as they came out of her skin.

Sirena raised her shirt to just under her

breasts and tugged the loose waistband of the sweatpants down over her hipbone. The bite marks had been deep gouges around her middle. Sven had sutured the worst of the gashes, but they were coming along nicely at this point.

So different than from just a few hours ago, when there had been very slow improvement, hindered by the magical energy drain. Now that the connection had been cut, Sirena was doing a lot better. Sven set to work, tugging gently on each stitch, cutting and pulling, doing his best not to hurt her.

Sirena didn't complain. She was a good patient, only stiffening once or twice when Sven moved too quickly and inadvertently caused her discomfort. He mentally kicked himself when that happened and redoubled his efforts to be gentle, but she never said a word of complaint. She was a trooper.

After he pulled the last stitch out of her creamy skin, Sven dropped the remnants of thread into the dish, then put his tools with the discarded threads for later sterilization, after he disposed of the waste. He used the gauze to swab the area with a topical disinfectant, examining her closely to be sure the skin was sealing itself. He was happy to see she was healing at a much quicker rate than before.

"I don't think you need a bandage on this at all anymore." He put the rest of the trash into the metal dish and looked up to meet her gaze.

"That was the worst of the wounds. The other spots are already knitting nicely, see?" She lifted her foot and tugged the hem of her sweatpants up to reveal what had been a nasty gash on her leg, then showed him her other foot, which had been in bad shape just a day or two ago. "The water did wonders. As did you." She lowered her feet back to the bed and reached for his hand.

It was the first time she'd touched him. Oh, he'd touched her a lot in the course of her treatment, but this was the first time she'd reached out and initiated contact between them. For some reason, that meant a lot to him. She held his hand and squeezed it as she looked into his eyes.

"Thank you for taking care of me when I was so weak. I'm not used to having anyone look out for me," she said, blushing a bit as she made the admission. "You saved my life."

The mood between them became intimate suddenly, as if they were the only two people left in the entire universe. All other sounds faded into the background. The only thing he could hear was the sound of her voice and the beat of their hearts.

"I'm glad I was there to help you, but I'm only sorry I didn't realize what was going on with your energy sooner." He would be kicking himself for a long time to come because he hadn't figured that out earlier.

"You couldn't have known. You even brought Gus in to check, and he didn't see it," she reminded him gently. "You did everything you could, and for that, I'm really grateful." She leaned closer and kissed his cheek.

His breath caught, and time slowed. Her lips were so soft against his cheek, like a butterfly caress. A thing of beauty and delicacy. What would she do if he turned his head and brushed her lips with his own? The bear inside prodded him to find out. Without giving it too much thought, he moved slowly enough for her to escape if that's what she wanted...but she didn't. She lingered, her lush lips near to his.

And then, they were kissing. A gentle

touch at first. A touch of seeking permission and cautious discovery, very unlike his usual experiences with the opposite sex. No, with Sirena, everything was bright and new. Different in the best possible way.

It was a tender kiss that morphed slowly into something hotter and even more mysterious as she allowed him to kiss her, and even joined in. Before his mind really registered what was going on, she'd thrown her arms around his neck and drawn him closer.

The chair was teetering on its front legs beneath him, but he followed where she led, fusing their torsos together, mirroring their lips. And then, he took it farther, his tongue licking out to taste her.

She moaned, and his blood caught fire. She leaned into him as he took her in his arms, trying to be as gentle as he could under the circumstances. The bear inside him wanted to pet her and comfort her. To show her how careful he could be, how much he cared for her.

Wait. The bear cared for her? Sven had thought it was his human side—the doctor part of him that wanted to help people—that had brought out his protective streak, but no. The bear was involved in this as deeply as his human half, which was a first.

Never before had the bear cared about anything other than immediate pleasure that could be gained from a female. It cared about dominance and sex for sex's sake. It hadn't ever urged him to be so careful with a particular woman, or cared for one so deeply.

It should have scared him shitless, but the truth was, it just felt right. Everything about finally having Sirena in his arms in passion felt good and pure and…like fate.

That thought rocked him even as her tongue licked out to duel with his. Oh, she was into this kiss as much as he was. He'd kick himself if she regretted it later, but for now, he couldn't deny himself the pleasure of her taste, the feel of her body under his hands and the softness of her in his arms.

A rustling sound from the doorway intruded, and for a moment, Sven wanted to just ignore it and hope it would go away, but the sound continued, breaking the spell that had nearly stopped time around them. He drew back, loving the well-kissed look on Sirena's beautiful face, the dilation of her mysterious eyes, the pleasure scent wafting from her soft skin. His bear wanted to rub himself all over her and bask in her delicate fragrance.

The rustling sounded again, and he looked up, over Sirena's shoulder. John Marshall, Alpha of Grizzly Cove, stood just outside the doorway, waving a paper in a fanning motion. The Alpha's expression was a mixture of surprise, concern and approval as he raised one eyebrow at Sven.

The bastard had seen everything, and Sven supposed he should be thankful for the Alpha's discretion. That waving paper had been designed to catch Sven's attention gently, without alarming Sirena. Sven would thank John later, after his inner bear got over the annoyance of being interrupted when he had a soft female in his arms.

John stepped backward a few feet, as Sven let Sirena go. Neither of them had spoken yet, but he knew he had only moments to set the scene John was providing, hoping to spare Sirena any embarrassment of being caught in the very improper act of necking with her doctor. Sven put a respectable distance between them.

She opened her mouth but didn't speak

when John deliberately made noise out in the clinic. Her gaze shot to the doorway as she sat on the bed. John came into view, walking heavily so he could be heard as Sven sat back on his chair.

"Glad to see you looking so much better, ma'am," John said with a quiet, friendly smile before turning his attention to Sven. "Got a minute, doc?"

Sven steadied his breathing and stood. "Sure thing, Alpha. What can I do for you?"

He paused only to send a last glance back at Sirena before leaving the room. Her face was attractively flushed, her eyes still holding a bit of the dazed look that had filled them just after he broke off kissing her. He wanted to see that look on her face again. Many times. Maybe for the rest of their lives.

CHAPTER EIGHT

Sven needed a minute to regroup after that life-altering kiss, but he didn't really have the time. John led the way into Sven's office and nodded for Sven to shut the door behind them, sealing them in the privacy of the small room.

Sven went to the small refrigerator he kept in one corner and grabbed a cold beverage. He needed to cool down. When he offered one to John, the Alpha shook his head, opting instead to take a seat in one of the chairs facing Sven's desk that he kept for visitors.

Good. That meant Sven could dive behind the illusory safety of his desk. He sat in his rolling office chair and tried to calm his raging arousal. Just a kiss from Sirena and he'd been all set to go off like a firework on the Fourth of July.

"What can I do for you, John?" Sven asked, sipping his icy cold drink.

"I set up the town council meeting as requested and managed a quick phone conversation with Drew's mom. She wouldn't say much about the discovery she made here earlier, but I take it, now that the connection to the leviathan, through its minion, has been cut, your patient is getting better?"

Sven nodded. "Much. I just took out the last of her stitches, and she's healing at the rate I would expect from a shifter now."

John hit Sven with that appraising raised-eyebrow look once again. "And the clinch I interrupted?"

"A new development," Sven admitted, not wanting to say much more. He wasn't sure what would come of the attraction he could no longer deny for Sirena. He'd have to sort a few things out with her first before he was ready to reveal anything to someone else, even the Alpha.

"Are you serious about her?"

He should've known John wouldn't just leave it alone. Sven shifted uncomfortably in his chair.

"I'm not sure what's going on yet, and even if I did, you wouldn't be the first to know. Sorry." Sven finished his drink and crushed the can in one hand, tossing it into the recycling bin he kept against the wall for just that purpose.

John laughed. "I wouldn't expect to be the first to know. That honor should go to your lady. But I hope you'd put me on the list somewhere."

Sven relented. "Yeah, you're on the list, but I'm not even sure what's happening yet, so give me some time to figure things out. It may be nothing."

"That didn't look like nothing," John observed.

It hadn't felt like nothing either, Sven admitted in the privacy of his own mind. A rather noncommittal "yeah," was all he said in reply to the Alpha's observation.

"So the meeting," John redirected them back onto the topic he'd come to discuss. "I've set it for four o'clock over at the town hall, in the conference room. If your patient is well enough, she deserves to be there. Mrs.

L is going to be discussing what she's learned about the leviathan from intervening with your lady friend. I'm not sure why she's being so mysterious, but priestesses have their ways, and I respect that." John stood from the visitor chair. "Will Sirena be well enough to make the meeting?"

"Probably. She's improving much more quickly now that the constant drain on her energy has been halted. I'll bring her over."

"Good. I'll see you both then." John walked out without further comment, and Sven was grateful for the Alpha's discretion. Sven had to get his own head screwed on straight first before he would feel at all comfortable in discussing his unprecedented reaction to Sirena.

*

Sirena was feeling a lot better as Sven escorted her out of the clinic for the first time since she'd arrived in Grizzly Cove. He wasn't letting her walk the short distance to the town hall. Instead, he led her at a slow pace, his hand solicitously under her elbow, to his car. It was a dark sedan, and that's about all she knew about cars. It had big doors and was easy to get into, even with her still somewhat stiff midsection. The open wounds from the sea monster's bite might be healing, but it would still take a bit of time for the tissue and muscle to recover fully.

She just thanked the benevolent Goddess that she *was* finally healing. Between Sven's medical interventions that had kept her alive to this point and the magical healing performed by the shaman and, most recently, by Drew's mother, the people of this town had really gone above and beyond for her. If she hadn't been disposed to like them before, Sirena had to admit that Grizzly Cove was a good place, filled with intrinsically good people who had been willing to go the extra mile in Sirena's time of need. She wouldn't forget that. Not ever.

And she would always remember the gentle care of the big polar bear shifter at her side. He'd been so concerned about her, and so bad at hiding his worry. It was almost funny now, but she couldn't yet laugh at the terrible danger she'd been in, even after she'd been brought here, to the comparative safety of the town. Sven had saved her life, of that she had no doubt.

And now, he acted the perfect gentleman,

helping her to his car and making sure she was all right at every step. It could have been annoying, but he was so sweet about it, she couldn't really take offense. Still, by the time he pulled up at the side door to the nearby town hall building, she was ready to show him that she wasn't as feeble as she had been just the day before.

She didn't wait for him to come around and open her door. Instead, she got out of the car on her own and did her best to march up the few steps to the door without wobbling. She was very pleased to find she felt much steadier on her feet than she had even an hour before. The fresh air seemed to be helping clear the last of the cobwebs out of her mind, and her body was following right along.

Sven caught up with her and gallantly opened the door for her. She entered the structure feeling a bit like a queen, with her manservant providing escort. It was a silly notion that made her smile as she got her first look at the town hall.

He'd brought them to the side of the building, very close to the meeting room. She could hear voices beyond an open doorway, through which cheerful light was spilling into the darkened hall. The sun was on its daily trip downward in the sky, and clouds had moved in, obscuring what little light was left. Sirena had noticed that the lights were on in every business they had passed on their short journey down Main Street.

She paused beside the open doorway, and Sven touched her arm.

"You okay?" he asked, his handsome face showing concern when she turned to look at him.

"Fine. I'm just not used to crowds anymore," she whispered.

"I'm right here," Sven reminded her, rubbing her arm in a show of support. "I'll be with you the whole time, and we can leave anytime you want. Just say the word."

She gave him a tight smile. He really was the most considerate male she had ever encountered. These bear shifters were proving to be nothing like she had expected.

She gave him a nod of thanks and took one of his hands for moral support as they entered the room together. The conversation in the room ceased and then started up again as two women rushed over, practically tackling Sirena where she stood. Her hunting party sisters, Grace and Jetty, were both there, smiling and hugging her in turn.

Sirena felt much more comfortable with them there. Between her mer sisters and Sven's presence, she didn't feel so out of place. The girls ushered her toward the large conference table, and before too much longer, they were all settled in seats around the massive wooden table.

Besides Grace and Jetty, Sirena recognized Jetty's mate, Drew, and his parents, Grace's mate, Jack, the Alpha bear, John, and his mate, Ursula, as well as her sister, Mellie. There were a few others she didn't recognize, but she soon realized that the bears weren't in charge of this particular meeting. No, this was all up to Mrs. Legine, the priestess. She sat at the focal point of the room, and all eyes turned toward her when she began to speak.

"Thank you all for coming," the priestess began, her voice calm, but filled with conviction and power. "I think you know why my husband and I came to town. We thought we were just going to have a nice visit with our son and new daughter-in-law and attend their mating celebration. Instead, I've discovered something I cannot ignore.

Neither can all of you."

Mrs. Legine looked down at her hands as her face went pale. She didn't seem ready to go on speaking, so the Alpha stepped in, his tone measured as he addressed the older woman.

"This has to do with Sirena's treatment? She looks a lot better than she did just yesterday. I'd say you'd worked another miracle, Mrs. L."

The priestess looked up at John, and her expression was tight.

"I broke a connection with the leviathan. Although she was injured by one of its servants, the magic that was drained from her was going mostly to feed the leviathan itself. It was still draining her. When I walked into the clinic, I found the doctor and his patient engaged in a screaming contest. Since I don't think that's his normal bedside manner, even though he *is* a polar bear, I surmised that something was influencing him. It wasn't a stretch to realize the leviathan was making him act that way. It was feeding off the anger through its minion's connection with Sirena."

Everybody at the table frowned, sending Sven dark looks. Sirena wanted to reach out to him, but wasn't sitting close enough to touch him with her hand, so she used words instead.

"It wasn't his fault," she tried to defend him.

"The hell it wasn't," John growled. "He's the doctor. He's supposed to notice things like that." John's accusatory tone and condemning gaze zeroed in on Sven. "How did you not see this?"

Sven felt anger build, but tamped it down. Now wasn't the time to argue with his friends.

"I had Gus check her out," Sven told them, trying not to sound defensive, "but he couldn't see whatever it was that was keeping her energy low. He thought she was free of the creature's taint." Some of the anger in the room dissipated at his explanation. Thank the Goddess.

"And the sad fact is, the leviathan's connection was something your shaman couldn't see," Mrs. Legine added. Sven watched the expressions around the table change to concern. "It kept draining her energy and prevented her healing."

"So why couldn't Gus sense the

connection?" John wanted to know. As the former unit leader and Alpha of the group, he had to keep up with his people's abilities and weaknesses. The fact that Gus had missed something so big was important to understand.

"I discussed this with him as soon as I left the clinic," Mrs. L told the group. "To me, the evidence suggests he couldn't see it because he's male." John frowned, and the others seemed equally stymied by the news as Drew's mom continued. "I learned a bit about the creature when I saw the way it was connected to Sirena." She paused, looking at each face gathered around the table. "I'm sorry to say, the leviathan is female. Which means...it can reproduce."

"Is that where all the smaller creatures came from?" John asked shrewdly.

"No. Not those. They seem to have come through from some distant realm with their leader, and will go back with it if we can banish it once again. Neither the leviathan, nor its smaller companions, belong in this realm. The thing is—if the creature gives birth here, in our realm, then the offspring will have a permanent connection with our oceans that can never be fully broken. If it gives birth before we can banish it, we're in even worse trouble than we are now."

The mer at the table looked almost distraught. It was Sirena who spoke first. "Does Nansee know?"

"I spoke to her privately just before I came here," Mrs. Legine replied, speaking directly to Sirena. "I thought she needed to know first, since it's your people who will be in the most danger if the worst happens."

Sirena nodded respectfully at the priestess, and Sven couldn't fault Mrs. L's logic. The mer were screwed if the leviathan unleashed its offspring on the world's oceans.

"The energy the creature used to keep its hooks in Sirena was female in nature, which is why your male shaman missed it. Not his fault. He just isn't equipped to visualize something so opposite to his nature," Drew's mother said, with a philosophical shrug. "Now that we're aware of the problem, I think, more than ever, that this new town needs a priestess—or a contingent of them—living here permanently. This town has only been in existence a short time and already you've garnered attention from Others, not all of whom are friendly. In fact,

I'd say there's a big ol' bullseye on Grizzly Cove because of all the powerful magical energy concentrated here in the form of your people. It's a target, but it's also your greatest strength," she went on. "You boys were trained to face all obstacles and overcome any foe. You're powerful, both as men and as bears, and you'll need to organize your defenses once again if you want to keep your town free of outside interference. The question is, do you fight for your right to live your lives in peace, on your own terms? Or do you disband and count Grizzly Cove as a failed experiment?"

Sven was surprised she'd even bothered to voice the question. To him, at least, the answer was obvious.

"We fight, of course," he said, looking around the table for support. Only John was frowning. One by one, everyone noticed.

After a pause, where he looked like he'd swallowed something distasteful, John spoke quietly.

"This is something we need to bring before the full council. Everyone needs to be heard and be allowed to make their own decisions based on the available information."

Mrs. Legine was nodding. "You're a good Alpha, John, but you need to move fast. The leviathan needs to be banished regardless, and it needs to happen soon, before it gains enough energy to reproduce." Drew's mom stood as if she was preparing to leave them. "In the meantime, I'm going to set some wheels in motion and call in spiritual reinforcements. Better find a place for them to stay, because I'm going to get some of my sister priestesses to come here and help us fight this thing."

She didn't wait for an answer, just marched out of the room, her mate with her. Drew's mom was on a mission, and the town was about to gain some more powerful new residents if Sven was any judge of her ability to make things happen.

CHAPTER NINE

"Well, I guess that's it for the meeting," John said, looking as nonplussed as everyone else in the room. "Not sure what else we can plan for defense until Mrs. L does her thing and we know what we're working with."

"What do you say to a barbeque at our place for dinner?" Urse invited everyone with a smile.

Sirena was impressed by the open and friendly manner of all the bear shifters, magic users and mer in the room. The community spirit seemed to be alive and well in Grizzly Cove, even with all the problems they'd been facing lately. She couldn't wait to be well enough to explore the town and the waters of the cove. She might not be up to hiking in the woods just yet, but she certainly felt well enough to accept the Alpha pair's generous dinner invitation.

Most of the group also accepted, except for Jetty and Drew, who had promised to spend time with Drew's parents. Sven was agreeable, and after a quick consultation to be sure she knew she could leave if she was feeling tired or unwell, Sven ushered Sirena out to his car again.

"Is there a liquor store in town?" she asked him as she buckled her seatbelt.

"Why? Are you a closet drinker?"

She looked up at him sharply, only to find he was teasing. His blue eyes danced with merriment, and she couldn't help but smile in response. He was easy to laugh with, she was discovering, which was something she hadn't expected of a bear shifter. She'd always thought they'd be really intense at all times, but she'd been wrong.

"No. I just thought it would be nice to bring a bottle of wine or something. I hate to show up for dinner at someone's house empty handed."

He seemed to think about it for a moment, then nodded as he started the car.

"We don't have a liquor store as such, but I have a few bottles at my place. You're right. It's only polite to bring something. I guess, being bachelors for so long, some of us have forgotten the niceties of polite society, but I wasn't raised in a cave, and I know Urse would appreciate the gesture." He pulled out of the gravel parking lot and headed down the street, toward the clinic. "Thanks for reminding me of my manners."

She hadn't meant to be a nag or anything, but the unexpected chance to get a glimpse of where Sven lived kept her silent on the subject. Instead, she quietly thanked him. "I can pay you back once they get the bank up and running. Thanks for going out of your way."

He pulled into the small lot next to the clinic, and only then did she notice the rocky path leading up the side of the hill into the woods. Sven's house must be up there, though it wasn't visible from the parking area.

"It's no trouble, and you don't owe me anything. I'd invite you up, but it's a bit of a climb, and you should still be taking it easy. I'll be right back." He put action to words and hustled out of the car and jogged up the path, disappearing into the trees.

Night was falling in earnest as the overcast day grayed into the dark of night. The woods were gloomy, but Sven reappeared a few minutes later, carrying two wine bottles. He wasn't jogging this time, she was glad to see. No sense shaking up the wine, right?

He rejoined her in the car and asked her to hold the bottles while he drove. They were chilled to the perfect temperature, she noticed, enjoying the coolness of the glass against her palms.

"Do you have a wine cooler?" she asked, surprised by the notion. But how else could she explain the perfectly chilled bottles?

"You don't have to sound so surprised." He shook his head, but there was a small grin on his lips as he answered he query.

"Sorry. It just…" She collected her thoughts and tried again. "I just didn't take you for a wine drinker."

"I developed a taste for it when I was in medical school. Most of the guys are beer drinkers, but a few of us like the finer things in life. When Zak gets his restaurant open, you'll see. That boy is a genius in the kitchen, and he has an in with the Maxwell Winery through his silent partner. Only the best vintages for our Cajun bear."

Sirena was impressed. Everyone knew how sought after Maxwell's wines were by humans and Other alike.

She looked at the labels on the two bottles he had handed her. Sure enough, they were Maxwell vintages. A burgundy and a pinot noir. Sirena looked forward to tasting them both, but they were expensive bottles.

"I'm definitely paying you back for this. These are some fine bottles of wine," she said, still examining the labels.

"No way, Sirena. You don't owe me a penny. I want to share these with friends, and I count you among my friends now." She turned to meet his gaze, but he stopped her protest. "Don't argue. This makes me happy, and I can always get more wine."

She couldn't really argue with that, and the way he'd said they were friends had started a warm glow in her center that made her bubble with joy. She hadn't felt that in a very long time, if ever, and she didn't say anything, preferring to bask in that strange, happy feeling while Sven drove them the short distance to John and Ursula's house, which was set back in the woods.

The house was lovely, what she could see of it. Sven ushered her around to the side of the structure where a large deck attached to a spacious kitchen via a sliding glass door. Everyone was already there, and they greeted Sven and Sirena warmly. Urse came forward and thanked them both for the wine.

Sirena felt a little like a freeloader, taking credit for Sven's wine, but Urse didn't give her a chance to object. She took the bottles and handed them off to her husband, making sure Sirena had a good seat at the table from which she could watch and participate in the gathering. Sven sat beside her, rather than going off with his friends, which made her feel better. Of course, Grace was there too, and Urse had thoughtfully seated them side by side, so Sven started a conversation with Jack, Grace's mate, while Grace and Sirena had a chance to catch up.

It wasn't too long before delicious aromas started wafting from the large grill off to one side of the deck. John was presiding over the smoking metal monster with the help of a couple of his friends while his mate went around pouring wine or handing out cold beer bottles. It was an impromptu gathering, which was all that much nicer for its spontaneity.

"You're looking a lot better, Sirena," Grace said quietly. "I was really worried about you there for a while."

"I know. I was worried myself," Sirena admitted. "But Drew's mother is pretty amazing, and whatever she did, it did the trick. Sven tried so hard. He's been really great through all of this. He even brought in his shaman friend, Gus, who is more than a little spooky." The girls shared a chuckle.

"Gus totally has this otherworldly vibe," Grace agreed. "But he's nice. On the whole, all the bears I've met here have been welcoming. Even the gruff ones, like Georgio."

"I haven't met him," Sirena said, sipping the wine, which was proving to be as excellent as its reputation.

"He doesn't come into town much. He was badly injured overseas and still has a few physical problems, but he's a heck of a nice guy when he's not being a grumbly bear." Grace sat back, enjoying her wine now that the main course was almost finished. The women were all done, but the men were still eating second or third helpings of the expertly cooked steak, ribs, chicken and fish

John had laid out. "Georgio even let me use his therapy pool when I first came here," Grace reminisced. "You know, you should probably get in the water tomorrow or whenever you feel up to it. A shift will sort you right out. At least it did for me. I swam for a half hour or so at Georgio's, and I felt like a new woman after. But you don't have to use a pool. The cove is safe now, thanks to Urse's magic spell."

The idea had a lot of merit. "I'll talk to Sven about it. He's got to know a spot where I won't be observed. I think I'm at the stage now where a shift and a swim might be just the thing."

Sven didn't really mean to eavesdrop on the mer ladies' conversation, but the idea of taking a swim with Sirena in her shifted form took hold of his imagination and wouldn't let go. Shifting often helped heal wounds— when done at the right time, of course. Judging by the way she was looking, Sirena was probably already at the stage where a shift would help her progress instead of hindering it.

And for his part, Sven hadn't had a moment to himself in days. He hadn't *gone polar*, as his friends jokingly called it, in too long. A little dip in the cove in his fur might be just the thing, but they had to be cautious and do it where they wouldn't be seen by any casual passersby. The road was open to all sorts of traffic now, and there was a chance—however small—that humans could be passing through at any time.

After dessert had been passed around and conversation had settled into low murmurs, Sven turned to Sirena during a lull in her near-constant chatter with her friend. "We can go for a swim later, if you're feeling up to it."

She turned to face him. They'd been seated next to each other throughout dinner but hadn't really had a chance for a private word until now.

"You heard what Grace said?"

Suddenly, he felt defensive. "Whoa. I wasn't eavesdropping, but I heard her talking about Georgio's therapy pool, and you both got a little loud at that point. I think everyone on this side of the table heard that part of your discussion."

Sirena shrugged as if it didn't matter. "I wasn't accusing you of anything. Our conversation wasn't intended to be private."

She gave him a gentle smile that made his insides go a little haywire. "I'd like to try for a swim, if you think you know a safe spot."

"I've got the perfect place."

An hour later, Sven pulled into the driveway of a construction site on a stretch of beach they'd recently set aside for a boathouse. The cove waters were deep enough in this spot to put in a boat ramp, as well as a community building that would serve several purposes.

"What is this place going to be when it's finished?" Sirena asked, eyeing the half-built structure in the dark. There were work lights around the construction site for safety reasons, and the bare bulbs burned all night, providing dim light here and there throughout the site.

"Up front here will be a gift shop with Grizzly Cove shirts and memorabilia for the tourists. Guide books to the galleries and other offerings too, once we get a few more businesses open. Sort of a visitors' center for newcomers to get the lay of the land."

They walked up the steps onto the decking that had been completed. The first floor already had floorboards, if not all the walls, but the project was moving along quickly.

"There's the boat ramp." Sven pointed to one side of the deck, where concrete had been poured during low tide to form a hard surface trailers could navigate easily. "And back here is the part your people will like best, I think."

He led her back around the main part of the building to a set of stairs leading down into the water. Alongside the stairs was a kind of slide—similar to the boat ramp, but made out of something smoother, more slippery, and graded on a more subtle angle.

"What's this?" she asked, looking at the arrangement with a dubious expression.

"Stairs for you to walk into the water when you're in human form and a ramp for those with tails to slide on. It's already coated with something that won't rub your scales the wrong way. The idea of the subtle grade was that you could go into or out of the water while still in shifted form. What do you think?"

"It's ingenious," she answered, examining the construction from every angle.

"And in a few days, there'll be lockers here for your people to store clothing and belongings. They're also going to install showers and other amenities. All completely private. For shifters only."

"Shifters?" she asked, looking at him with one raised eyebrow and a sexy little smile on her face. "Not just mer?"

"Well, some of us bears like the water too."

"You don't say?" Her smile was challenging and a bit flirty. Sven moved closer to her. He couldn't help himself. "Are you going to swim tonight too?"

In answer, Sven pulled his sweater over his head and let it drop onto the decking beneath their feet. Nobody could see them from the road, even though the building wasn't complete. There was enough privacy for them to get into the water from here, and the dark of the night would hide them once they entered the water.

"My furry side needs to stretch his muscles a bit, and he loves the water as much as I do. Do you mind sharing the water with a white bear? I promise I won't bite...unless you want me to." His voice dipped low, answering the flirtatious mood she had introduced.

Thankfully, she didn't seem to be backing

away. If anything, she was moving closer as her smile deepened.

"Keep your teeth to yourself, bear," she teased, pushing one hand against his chest. Little sparks ignited against his skin where she touched, and he tried hard not to gasp.

Their magic had been like this since the beginning—a little at odds, but rubbing along deliciously together when they touched. Of course, she'd been at such low energy before, whenever he'd touched her, he'd only felt an echo of the power that sparked between them now.

"At least until you're invited," she went on, pushing past him toward the stairs. Then, without another word, she loosed her long hair until it lay around her shoulders in a tumbling mass.

Keeping her back to him, she performed a sort of strip-tease while Sven stood there, his mouth open in surprise and utter awe. He'd seen her naked before, but she'd been injured at the time and near death. He'd known she was beautiful, but now, here, in the moonlight with the sparkling ripples of water reflecting the mellow light of the moon onto her skin... She was the Goddess made flesh. The most beautiful woman on

Earth, in heaven or among the stars. She was magic, personified.

And he wanted her. Oh, how he wanted her.

With a giggle, she dove into the water before shifting and slid deep into the dark waters of the cove. Sven, released from the spell she had cast over him that had made him freeze into motionlessness, sprang forward to the edge of the stairs. He tried to look for her beneath the lapping water, but didn't see a single trace of her passage until she surfaced, her mer form having taken hold while she'd been out of sight.

She was even more beautiful, if such a thing was possible. Her fragile human skin had been replaced by a flexible armor of pearlescent scales, fine and colorful around her face, and farther down her luscious body, hiding her nipples beneath their protective curves. He couldn't see much of her tail beneath the water, but he did note her wet hair slicked back from her forehead to trail down her back and into the water where it spread out, flowing freely.

She was breathtaking. Truly stunning.

"So what about it, doctor?" she asked, smiling slightly. "I've never seen a polar bear up close."

"You're about to," he said, knowing his voice was filled with the growl of his inner bear. She didn't seem to mind. In fact, her smile broadened, her scales glistening faintly in the reflected moonlight.

Sven stripped, not bothering to hide his body from her. He was a shifter, after all.

Make that an *aroused* shifter. Still, she didn't seem to mind that either.

CHAPTER TEN

Sirena had to catch her breath when Sven dropped trou right in front of her. The man had no shame. Of course, with a body like his, there was absolutely no need for shame. In fact, his tall, lean, muscular form was a living work of art, and his erection... Well, it made her speechless. And greedy.

She was about to overheat, turning the water to steam around her, when the most amazing thing happened. All that buff hotness was surrounded by a swirling snowstorm of white-hot magical energy that made her blink. When the nearly blinding flash ended, Sven was gone, and a massive—downright giant—polar bear stood in his place.

"Wow," she breathed, watching him as he watched her.

His eyes had changed shape slightly, but the blueness of them was the same, as was the snapping intelligence. She had no doubt it was Sven behind that furry muzzle and the row of razor-sharp teeth.

The claws were pretty impressive too, she thought as he walked slowly toward the slide. There was a somewhat devilish cast to his features when he plopped himself down on the slick surface and let gravity do its thing. He entered the water with a little splash, and she submerged, wanting to keep an eye on the giant predator that had just joined her in the waters of the cove.

She spotted him immediately, keeping a respectful distance, as if he understood her trepidation. She hadn't been in the water since her injury, and sharing space with a dangerous beast with sharp teeth—even though she knew intellectually that it was Sven and not the leviathan—was bringing up some unresolved issues she hadn't really realized she had.

That Sven seemed to have taken it into consideration was another thing she had to admire about him. With him keeping a decent distance between them, she was able to calm down and overcome the worst of her fear.

As her panic began to subside, she realized the shift had done wonders for her overall wellbeing. She took a quick moment to take stock of her injuries and was pleased to find that all the little wounds that had been left were now gone in the flash of her scales. The most serious of the injuries were still a bit tender, but much better than they had been. She could flex and bend her midsection in ways she hadn't been able to just moments ago, in her human form.

Shifting had definitely done its part in her healing, and she felt joy bubble up inside her for the first time since being hurt. Sven had brought her here. He'd stayed with her while she'd been at her lowest point and willed her to live. He'd given her the time and the space she'd needed to make a comeback, and she would always be thankful to whatever benevolent power had landed her in his care.

Thinking of him, she looked at his bear form with all due consideration. He was an absolute monster. White in the sparkling waters of the cove. His fur waving in the current as his paws acted like massive clawed paddles, helping him stay in position, several yards away, watching her. He seemed to be waiting for her to make the first move. He also seemed to be observing her as carefully as she did him, but she didn't mind. She took it as yet another sign that the good doctor was there for her, watching over her recovery.

Although…the man had been very aroused just a few moments ago. *Impressively* aroused, in fact. Sirena hadn't seen a male like that in…well…ever. Sven truly was a specimen to behold. Long, lean, powerful, and just made to please a woman, she'd bet.

That little part of her that had always seen how attractive the doctor was sparked in interest once more. Now that she was feeling better and had overcome some of her dislike of him—which was really dislike of being so ill that he had to look after her—the attraction had flared once more. It was pretty clear, based on the evidence, that he was interested too.

Sirena began to think about Sven in a purely carnal way that would have made her human skin turn red with a flush of excitement. She hoped her scales hid the naughty direction her thoughts had taken, but she couldn't be sure. The polar bear doctor had proven very perceptive of the past few days.

With a playful flick of her tail, she turned and headed out into the cove, looking back at him and waving him onward, inviting him to join her. She would deal with the attraction later. For now, her mer side wanted to glory in the freedom of the water and learn the new environment of the cove.

She also sensed others from her pod not too far away. The mer were a social people when they gathered together, though the vastness of their domain in the oceans often had them swimming in smaller groups. Still, when the pod gathered, there was usually a party, and the joyful vibrations of the water told her the young and old alike were having a good time in their new playground of the cove.

Sirena moved out ahead, but Sven didn't waste much time, swimming strongly a few yards behind and to one side of her. He was surprisingly agile in the water for such a large beast. She hadn't really expected how at home he was in her element, though he did have to surface occasionally for air, where she could just use her gills.

The cove wasn't terribly deep along the edges, but as she moved deeper into the peaceful waters, she was surprised by the rocky drop-offs and craggy areas that would make excellent dwellings for those with young to protect. In fact, as she swam along, she saw that several of the areas she spotted were showing signs of new habitation. It looked to her like the mer had moved in and were working toward making a home in the tranquil waters of Grizzly Cove.

Sirena felt so much better than she had just an hour ago. Shifting had definitely been a good idea. Having Sven along as a giant furry chaperone seemed odd at first, but as she got used to his looming presence near her in the water, she began to feel a sense of safety she had seldom felt in the open ocean.

Part of it was the cove itself. There was a tranquil peace about the waters here that could only be described as magical. The spell that had been cast over this water made it inviting and even sort of *welcoming* to the mer, and Sirena wasn't immune to the soothing effects of the water here. But a large part of the feeling of security that warmed her was Sven himself. He made no overt moves, taking his cues from her, but if the least little thing looked like it might cause her trouble—a stray stand of tall kelp, or a tangle of sea grass—he was there, batting it back, out of her way.

She felt like a princess. Or some kind of celebrity who had handlers and security to ease their way through life. With Sven around, she felt like nothing would ever harm her again. Not if he had anything to say about it.

The fierce beast with teeth and claws had, at first, brought back memories of terror. Her response had morphed, though, into feelings of protection and care. She knew, in her deepest heart, that Sven would never turn those lethal aspects of his dual nature on her. On the contrary, he'd use his attributes and abilities to protect her, if at all possible.

She missed her weapons. Usually, when she swam out with her hunting party, she carried several blades and her spear. She'd have to ask what had happened to them later. She assumed the spear, at least, had been lost, because the last time she'd seen it, it had been sticking out of the creature that had attacked her, buried deep in its ghastly hide.

The fact that the beast hadn't even flinched when she'd hit it with all her might made Sirena want to shudder, but she refused to ruin this moonlit swim with thoughts of that terrible battle. That was over and done. She had to live for this moment, this beautiful evening with a man who intrigued her more and more.

As she thought that, Sven swam up beside her, closer now, but still giving her space. He was a big white blur of fur and motion. He seemed to be motioning over to the right, beckoning her to follow. Curious, she swam in the direction he led her in, wondering what he wanted to show her.

It wasn't long before she spotted the secluded spot some of her people appeared to have chosen as a gathering place. The water was deep here, but Sven seemed to manage it for reasonable periods of time, though he had to surface now and again to take a breath. That he'd known where to find her people told her he'd been out here before, swimming reconnaissance, perhaps? Or maybe the leader of the pod, Nansee, had given the bears the information for some reason.

That wasn't the usual way. Mer were secretive and tried to remain hidden at all times in the open ocean, but this whole situation wasn't normal. The mer had never worked with a shifter group on this scale before, to Sirena's knowledge. And, of course, nothing like Grizzly Cove had been attempted before either, that she knew. So, perhaps, they were all just muddling along, making up the rules about how this relationship between their peoples would work, as it happened.

Sirena swam into the gathering place, grateful to see a few folks she knew. None of her hunting party were present, but she received nods of welcome and even the brush of a webbed hand or two along her tail fin from a few of those she counted as friends. Mer weren't terribly demonstrative in their scaled form, but she felt the love from her people, and the pleasure they took in seeing her well and able to swim once more.

They were a little wary of the giant polar bear, but seemed more used to seeing him— or those like him—than she would have expected. Then again, the others had been swimming in the cove since day one and probably knew the bears here a lot better than she did at this point. Maybe some of the other furries liked swimming too. For such large land predators, they certainly seemed well able to adapt to the water environment, at least based on what she had observed with Sven. If grizzlies were as aquatic as polar bears, perhaps the mer had been swimming with the big furry guardians of the cove for a while now.

Sven left her below, rising to breathe. He lingered on the surface for a bit, giving her time to reacquaint herself with her people. He was a thoughtful man, a powerful bear, and a kind protector. The more she was around him, the more she liked him.

Sirena stayed below for a bit, swimming with her pod-mates and seeing the work they'd done already to transform this part of the cove. She was impressed with how perfect the natural landscape of the cove had been to start with and what her people had managed to do in such a short time to make it even more hospitable to their kind.

Sooner than she would have liked, she started to feel the fatigue that seemed never far away from her lately. It wasn't nearly as bad as it had been, but she wasn't used to swimming long distances now, after being laid up for so long. She'd have to work on rebuilding her stamina—but not tonight.

Sirena took her leave of the gathering place and rose to the surface, using her tail to propel her on a leisurely path toward the moonlight that filtered down into the clear waters of the cove. The disc of the moon shone bright above her, more visible the higher she rose in the water, until finally, she broke the surface to find it shining down over her.

Mother Moon was in fine form tonight, Sirena thought, sending a prayer of thanks toward what her people thought of as one of the many faces of the Goddess. She Who Ruled the Tides was a powerful force in their world. One to be revered and respected for all her awesome beauty.

Basking in the moonlight, Sirena floated for a bit, knowing her companion bear wasn't far away. In fact, she could feel his magical energy watching over her, swimming light circles around her floating form. She'd been afraid of Sven at first, but not because she really thought he would ever harm her. No, it had been leftover fear of sharp teeth and agony that had assailed her, but was quickly dealt with in the face of Sven's goodness and willingness to give her space.

He let her swim free, though he was a protective presence the whole time. She supposed, just a few weeks ago, she might've been annoyed by the idea. She'd been independent to a fault, mad at the world and most of the men in it. But a lot had changed since then. She'd been reminded of her own mortality and had come close to succumbing to the soul-stealing leviathan.

Sven had refused to give up on her. He'd brought in specialists and hadn't stopped until he'd found a solution for her. He'd been her guardian angel, in a way, and she would never be able to thank him enough for believing that she could be healed. His faith had kept her going, even when she'd felt about ready to give up on herself.

His bear form was enchanting—at least from a distance. She decided it was time to see how their magics would react to each other. Swimming with purpose, instead of just floating, she moved closer to the white bear.

Rather than repulsing each other, as opposing magics often did, she felt drawn to him. As she drew closer to him, their magics

140

pulled them together in a way she'd never really experienced. Like a gentle whirlpool, spinning her close to him as they both tread water in the peaceful cove, under the light of the Goddess moon.

Sirena shifted her face so that she could speak through human teeth rather than her sharper, pointier mer teeth. Her scales flowed away, down her neck, halting at the water line, leaving her in human form from there upward. Mer were experts at shifting only parts of their bodies so as to pass for human when the need arose. They practiced it from a young age.

The bear tilted his head, watching her with those piercing blue eyes, then a flash of white snow energy made her look away. When she looked back, the bear had become the man. Sven tread water in human form, not three feet from her, and he was very, very naked. *Yum.*

"You're a great swimmer," she told him.

"Looks like shifting did you good," Sven said, smiling at her in the moonlight.

"It worked wonders. I feel almost back to my old self again. I'll just have to work on my stamina a bit."

His brows drew together in concern. "Are

you okay to swim back?"

She moved closer, putting her hand on his shoulder. She shifted her scales back so she could feel his warm muscle under her human fingertips.

"I'm fine. Just not as strong as I was before being injured. But it'll come back. I'm certain of it now. A little work and a lot of swimming will have me back in fighting form in no time."

"Just don't overdo it. I don't want to see you back in my infirmary for a good long time." He didn't move away. In fact, it seemed he was infinitesimally closer, and getting more so all the time.

Sirena dared greatly, putting her other hand on his other shoulder. It wouldn't take much to slide her hands up around his neck. The motion of her tail kept her upright and floating, but he had to use his hands and feet.

"What if I like your infirmary?" She wasn't very good at pouting or playing the ingénue, but she was giving at her best shot, and it seemed to be working, judging by the hungry look in his eyes. "Besides...where am I going to sleep tonight if you don't let me come back? I don't have a place yet in this town, and I'm not really up to staying in the water just yet."

"What if I said you can stay at my place?" His voice had dropped down low, and there was a definite rumble of his bear in it. *Sexy.*

"Do you have a guest room, or would I have to share with you?" Oh, yeah. She would *love* to share his bed, and just in case he didn't recognize her signals yet, she slipped her fingers up over his shoulders and around his neck. His thick golden hair was slick against her hands at his nape, and it felt divine.

"You can sleep wherever you like in my den, Sirena. I won't quibble." He stared down into her eyes, his expression suddenly serious. "And I need you to know that you don't owe me any...favors...for helping you. My services come with absolutely no strings attached."

She met his gaze, feeling bolder than she ever had. Something about Sven brought out the wild woman in her soul and gave her a confidence she'd never quite had with any other man. It was a heady feeling.

"Got it, doc. No strings. And you should know that my...uh...services are the same. I do what I want, when I want, with who I want—as long as the other party shares my interest." She decided to stop beating around the bush. "Look, Sven. I like you. I appreciate what you did for me, but that's about as far as it goes on that score. Anything else is strictly between you and me. Because I feel an…attraction. I mean, look at us."

She removed one hand from his nape and trailed her fingers down over his shoulder and onto his chest. Wherever she touched, little sparks of magic glowed between them.

"Our magic likes each other. We're different, but if this is anything to go by, we're compatible," she went on. "I've never sparked with anyone like this before. Don't you feel it too?"

Sven seemed mesmerized, watching the progress of her fingers on his chest. "I didn't want to get my hopes up. I wasn't sure you recognized this…thing…drawing us together. I've felt it since the moment I first saw you, Sirena." His gaze rose to meet hers, and she read the honesty and passion there. It was a mirror for her own feelings.

That was it. She reached upward and kissed him. He seemed surprised at first, but then took over, showing her all the pent-up passion within him. It was a match for hers...and then some. Then again, she'd been at such low energy since they first met, until now, that she was playing catch-up to him on the attraction front. Now that she was almost completely well, though, she found him almost completely irresistible.

His kiss set her on fire, and when they drew apart, she was surprised to find the waters of the cove hadn't turned to steam around them.

"Shall we adjourn this 'til we get back on terra firma?" Sven's arched eyebrow and inviting smile made her want to jump him, but since he was a land dweller and she was still somewhat weak, that would best be accomplished out of the water.

"I would ask *your place or mine*, but I don't have a place here yet," she said, aiming for a joke, but hitting a bit of a raw nerve instead.

She hadn't picked out a spot in the cove or found a real place of her own on land yet either. She was rootless and unsure where she belonged...except she knew one thing for certain. For the next few hours at least, she belonged wherever Sven was.

"*Mi casa es su casa,*" he intoned, his smile widening. "What do you say?"

"I say, what are we waiting for?" She laughed as she swam away from him, back toward the half-finished building on shore.

She kept looking back to see the long, lean, muscular lines of his human form swimming strongly in her wake. He was pretty devastating in both his forms and looked about as at home in the water as a land dweller could be. That was definitely a big point in his favor as far as she was concerned.

CHAPTER ELEVEN

Sven didn't want to count his chickens before they hatched, or otherwise take anything for granted, but it sure sounded like he was about to get lucky with the beautiful mermaid who had been plaguing his thoughts since the moment he'd first seen her. *Getting lucky*, though, didn't really cover it. That was a silly phrase he discarded almost as soon as it entered his mind. It wasn't just *lucky*. It was more like *blessed*. Singled out by the Goddess for a special gift. Getting something he was almost afraid to want too much because it felt too important.

Oh, yeah…there was nothing light or lucky about this. If it happened. For, if

Sirena agreed to share his bed, he knew deep down in his heart, he would never be the same. His world would shift on its axis, and he would look at everything with a new perspective.

Or so he believed. And feared. And anticipated. It was a heady feeling, this fizzing joy of hesitant anticipation bubbling through his veins. He hadn't felt like this since he'd been a child—if then.

Something momentous was about to happen. Maybe. If she didn't change her mind.

He cut through the water, stretching out his arms to keep up with his pretty mermaid. Her tail was just about the prettiest thing he'd ever seen, and she'd been right about the way their magic sparked. His bear had loved swimming with her, and the bear had felt nothing but attraction, care and protectiveness toward her. His bear side had wanted to play with her, not hunt, which was a relief. He'd been half afraid the first meeting of their shifter sides wouldn't go quite this well, but he guessed he should have known.

After all, he was truly beginning to believe that—odd as it seemed—Sirena just might be his mate. Tonight would tell. He suspected he'd know for certain after they joined for the first time. If it was going to be as special as he suspected, he might just spend the rest of his life with this one woman...and count himself blessed to do so. If she agreed, that is.

And if she didn't agree, he'd spend the rest of his life trying to convince her to be his and his alone. There were worse ways to spend one's remaining decades. Of course, if she felt the same... Well, then. They could spend those decades making babies, playing in the surf, and generally living happily ever after.

Caught up in the daydream of what might be, he had to shake himself when they neared shore. His senses were sharper in his bear form, but he was still able to sniff out the presence of others in the boathouse. Concerned, he powered through the water, drawing even with, and then overtaking, Sirena.

She shot him a bemused look as he sped past her, and he knew she let him pass, because even tired, with that tail of hers, she could have easily outpaced him in the water. Perhaps she sensed something too. Or maybe not. He'd have to ask her later so he could better assess her abilities. If they were going to be mates, he'd have to know all her weaknesses and strengths, so as to protect her.

For now, though, he let that startling thought slide. Right now, he had to find out exactly who was waiting in the boathouse. If there was danger, he would face it. He would protect his mate no matter what.

The scents of the water and the life therein obscured the identifying markers that normally would have told him exactly who was waiting on shore. Plus, the breeze wasn't cooperating. It was blowing in the opposite direction, in fact. Only a small contrary zephyr had brought him the hint of scent that had alerted him.

As he drew closer to shore, he was able to see that there was more than one figure near the stairs that led into the water from the shadows of the boathouse. A set of smaller bodies looked decidedly female in outline, while a much larger shape looming behind them seemed more familiar.

If Sven had to guess, he'd say it was most likely John, the Alpha, showing two of their mermaid guests the new water entry that had only just been declared safe by the work crews that day. In fact, Sven and Sirena had probably been the first to use it without supervision.

Ratcheting down his sense of alarm, Sven tried to set himself into watch mode. He would still be hyperaware of any threat to Sirena, but having assessed the situation as peaceful, he could relax just the tiniest bit. Still, Sven went ashore first, using the stairs in a rapid approach as the two females waiting there moved back to make way for his powerful approach.

The Alpha stood his ground, of course. John and Sven had worked and fought together for many years. They knew each other well and understood most actions without need for explanation. John held up one hand, giving the military hand signal to reassure Sven that all was well and no danger lay in wait.

Sven nodded to John, then to the women before moving off to one side to speak in low tones with John. He kept an eye on Sirena's slower rise out of the water, but she was immediately surrounded by her two friends, who seemed to want to make a friendly fuss over her. It was a good thing to have friends to count on, and Sven watched indulgently as the two females shielded Sirena from male eyes while she dried off and dressed on the other side of the large open room.

Sirena was a bit hesitant to rise out of the water with the Alpha bear looking on, but she saw her opportunity when Sven went on ahead and took the Alpha off to one side. Beth and Janice were waiting too and understood her modesty. Although they swam around in their scales all the time without clothing, the scales themselves were a sort of shield that hid most of what humans tried to hide with fabric.

Land shifters might be comfortable with nudity—and it was clear Sven had no real modesty when he leapt out of the water, giving Beth and Janice a full frontal view without even seeming to realize it—but mer were different. They shifted in private most of the time, and only when heading in and out of the water, which, for Sirena, wasn't often. She'd decided a few years ago to make her home in the ocean, for now, and only left it a couple of times a year, to visit her folks.

It was too risky to go in and out of the water too frequently. With so many humans around, with their technology—satellites, surveillance cameras, and even recreational drones that could take damning photos—it was getting riskier to shift all the time. Even the dark of night couldn't hide much anymore. Not with infrared cameras and commercially available night vision devices that turned dark to light.

That's why this protected boathouse was such a good idea. Her people could go from land to sea without being observed, which was ideal. Still, the nudity would take some getting used to. Of course, from what she'd seen of the residents of Grizzly Cove, not one of them had any reason to be modest.

Muscled and lean, the men around here were a sight to behold when clothed. Seeing them in the nude was no hardship to women who'd been just a bit lonely living under the waves for so long. Most of the few mermen in their pod were all paired up with permanent mates and children, so there wasn't a whole lot of dating action in their community.

Sirena sensed that was all about to change, now that they had the luxury of a batch of handsome male shifters so nearby. Two of her friends had already found their mates among the bears, and Sirena thought a few more might be so blessed in the months to come. And if they didn't find their one true loves, they at least could date some hot guys and have a little fun while they waited to find their mates.

She dressed quickly with Beth and Janice providing a shield of sorts, but the Alpha bear was polite and turned his gaze away even before she rose from the water. He was newly mated and, from all evidence, deeply in love with his wife, so Sirena supposed he didn't need to ogle other women. Oddly enough, Sirena didn't mind Sven's gaze so much. In fact, some little devil of intrigue wanted to show him what was on offer, even with the audience.

But maybe the presence of her friends was a good thing. It would keep her from throwing herself at the doctor—at least for a little while longer. If she was alone with Sven again, she didn't think she'd be able to stop herself. She wanted him bad, and after their frolic in the sea where her mer side got to know his furry self, she would not be denied. Their magic sparked in sultry, seductive ways that must be explored. Soon.

"You're looking so much better, Sirena," Janice offered, holding out Sirena's sweater. "How do you feel?"

"Much better. Still not up to full steam as far as my stamina goes, but the shift did wonders for my wounds," Sirena admitted, bending down to put on her shoes.

Beth helped, crouching down in front of Sirena. "Are you sure you should be so chummy with the bear?" Beth whispered.

"Beth…" Sirena felt the undercurrents of concern tinged with suspicion in her friend's voice.

Beth was a strange one. Youngest of the hunting party, Beth was shy and very needy for someone who had only joined the group the year before. Sometimes, Sirena wondered if Beth had ever known love, since the other woman seemed to find it so hard to express that emotion even in friendship. It was kind of sad, really, and Sirena was extra patient with Beth because she felt a bit sorry for her, but she found herself resenting Beth's butting in where Sven was concerned.

"Look. He saved my life. I have absolutely no doubt about that. Without Sven, I'd have been dead weeks ago," Sirena told her honestly, keeping her voice down to a whisper.

She didn't want Sven to know that any of her friends had doubts about him. It was insulting, for one thing. Especially after all he'd done for her and her people.

"Maybe so, but that doesn't mean—" Beth began, but Sirena cut her off.

"I like him, Beth. He's a good man. End of story."

Sirena ended the topic by finishing with her shoes and standing. Beth had to stand as well, and Sirena wouldn't entertain any more questions or doubts about Sven. She effectively terminated the conversation by squaring her shoulders and striding over to where Sven and John stood, still talking in low tones.

She didn't wait, but walked right up and joined the duo, greeting John with a friendly smile. Sven seemed to understand that there'd been some byplay among her and Beth and immediately made room for her, welcoming her into their circle.

"I'm glad to see you up and around, ma'am," John said, nodding politely.

"Thank you, Alpha. I'm much better for having shifted, and it's thanks to your doctor friend here that I got to this point at all. If Sven hadn't kept me going until Mrs. Legine could work her magic, I never would have made it." Sirena wanted the bear leader to know she was fully aware of how much the community of Grizzly Cove—and Sven, in particular—had done to keep her alive.

Sven ducked his head slightly, as if embarrassed by her praise, but John merely nodded. "I'm glad he could help you," he said, giving her a look of understanding that said much more than his words. "And if there's anything else we can help you with as you complete your recovery, be sure to let one of us know. You were injured protecting your people, and that's something we can not only understand, but respect." The bear leader surprised her with his words. "This town was founded around our old military unit. We're all soldiers at heart, and I definitely recognize that warrior spirit in you, Sirena. When you're up to it, I'd like to talk to you about improving security for the cove itself. We've got the land covered, but it's clear we need to step up our monitoring of the water approaches. I've already begun talks with your leader on this, but I'd like to have you on the committee, if you're willing." Pleased by his offer, Sirena nodded in response. "You too, Sven," John added, looking from Sirena to the doctor standing at her side, and back again, his eyes lighting with humor. "Nobody likes cold water swimming as much as our furry white friend here."

Sirena giggled. That was the only word for the joyous sound that came straight from her chest...in the vicinity of her heart. These bears made her feel not only welcome, but part of something much bigger than her hunting party, or even her pod. They made her feel part of the land-dwelling world in a way she never had, even if she'd been born and raised mostly on land.

"I'd be honored, Alpha. Thank you for asking," she vocalized her agreement, just so he'd know for certain how she felt.

To be honest, she was a little overwhelmed by the emotion his offer inspired. She'd never expected to be so well received by this scary group of land shifters, but they'd all but rolled out the red carpet for her and her people. Maybe they weren't quite as scary as they'd feared.

"I was just showing the sea stairs and slide to your friends," John said, moving closer to the other two women who were watching them. "What do you think?"

"It's a great idea," Sirena said without hesitation. "And this private area in which to enter and leave the water is perfect."

"It's a little public," Beth chimed in, joining the conversation, her forehead wrinkled in a frown.

"We're not used to shifting in front of others," Sirena explained when John seemed confused. "But it's not that big a deal," she added, willing her friends to play along. The bears were being so nice, and it was *their* town, after all. "Just being able to shift out view of satellites, airplanes, drones and tourists will be very welcome."

John scratched his cheek. "I never really thought about it before, but most of the coastline is very exposed. Even if you shift upstream and swim down one of the tributaries, you'd still be exposed quite a bit. Must be more difficult for you folk than I realized."

Sirena shrugged and smiled at the Alpha. "We manage. We just don't shift as often as you bears do, since it's tricky to get from land to sea and vice versa without risk of being seen. Even at night. Which is why this boathouse is ideal."

The conversation drifted at that point, and Sirena began to feel the fatigue that was just starting to really catch up to her. She sort of tuned out the others, who kept talking about the boathouse and its attributes. Sven came to her side and put an arm around her waist, supporting her as she rested her head against his shoulder. It felt good to lean on someone—quite literally—for a change. Sven was tall and strong, and she felt like she fit against him like they were made to go together.

"My former patient needs her rest," Sven put in when there was an opening in the ongoing conversation between the other three. "Good night all."

Sirena received a few questioning looks from her friends, but John merely smiled and wished her a good night as Sven whisked her out of there with less fuss than she'd expected.

CHAPTER TWELVE

When they pulled into the clinic parking lot, Sven paused, stopping the car just inside the entrance to the lot.

"Where to? Your old room or my place? I leave it up to you." He kept his hands on the steering wheel and turned just his head to look at her as his words faded.

She was tired, but not *that* tired. The flame Sven had kindled in her blood was still flaring strong, and she wanted to explore their attraction. Daring greatly, she whispered. "Your place."

Sven gave her a small grin and turned his attention back to the wheel. Instead of parking close to the clinic entrance, he

161

moved his vehicle back toward the area where she'd seen him go up the pathway when he'd fetched the wine just an hour or so earlier. It seemed like longer than that. In fact, she felt like she'd known him—or been waiting for him—all her life.

He parked the car in a secluded space that had a *reserved* sign on it. Not that it was necessary. His was the only car in the lot at the moment. But these bears were planners, and they had probably set up the clinic lot with the future in mind when the town would be bigger and the town doctor and clinic would be busier.

Sven opened her door for her and ushered her toward the pathway that led...somewhere. The trees were dense here and created a living canopy over the tops of their heads. If it hadn't been dark out, the path would still have been shaded by the treetops. There were no lights. Most shifters could see very well in the dark, so they weren't strictly necessary, though if the bears wanted to maintain a semblance of humanity, she might recommend they put some in, just for appearances sake.

Mer had gotten very good at blending in over the years living closely alongside humans on the coasts of various countries. Other shifters tended to keep to the wild places, which were less populated by humans. This Grizzly Cove experiment, if it progressed to where they opened up the town even more to human foot traffic, would be quite a challenge—hiding a large concentration of shifters all together, in plain sight. Sirena knew her people could help the bears there, but that talk was for later. Tonight was all about just the two of them.

"Are you okay with the climb? It's not too steep for you?" Sven asked solicitously.

"I'm fine. I didn't realize how far up the slope your house was. It's really hidden quite well from the clinic." She looked behind her and saw that the parking lot was out of sight, around a slight bend.

"The clinic is my public space, but my den is private," he explained. "Only those I invite come here. Before this town, most of us would have been considered loners, and we still like our space."

"I can see that," she said, nodding toward the house just coming into view around another subtle bend in the pathway. "Wow." She stopped short just to take it in as the house was fully revealed. "That's gorgeous."

163

"I'm glad you like it. I designed it, though some of the guys helped me build it. I'm not as good a carpenter as some of the others," he admitted, showing a bit of humility. "Come on, I'll show you inside."

He led the way into the house, pausing to see her reaction when he turned on the gentle lighting. The impact was magnificent. The place had been built on an open concept, and the main area was done in what she could only describe as ocean colors—rich greens, a multitude of blues and frothy whites. It was a mermaid's dream. Or a polar bear's, apparently.

"This is..." She trailed off as she moved into the living room, turning in a circle to take in the high ceilinged area. "It's beautiful, Sven."

"I'm glad you like it." He stood a few feet away, watching her. The moment stretched until she looked back at him.

"It's the colors of the oceans," she said quietly, meeting his gaze.

"The northern oceans, to be exact," he stated, stalking quietly closer, holding her gaze, moving in that slow, sexy, silent way of his. "The Bering Sea. The Arctic Circle. Places my bear feels at home. This is his den as much as it's my home, and we both want you to be comfortable here."

"I bet you say that to all the girls." She couldn't help the catty comment.

The thought of Sven with any other woman made her turn feral. Especially in this lovely house that looked as if it had been built especially for her. If she could have dreamed about the perfect place to live, this would be very close to her ideal. It was truly lovely. And secluded, despite being close to the center of the small town.

"Actually…" Sven stood right in front of her and touched her hair with the barest brush of his fingertips, allowing a few strands to curl around his hand. "I've never brought a woman here. You're the first, Sirena. In so many ways, you're an original. A one-of-a-kind in my experience. I feel like everything is fresh and new with you…and…special."

Her breath caught. Unless her instincts were way off, he was completely serious. And his words mirrored thoughts she'd been having about him. She'd been with other men, but somehow, everything about Sven was different. Outside her experience. Completely original, like he'd said.

What did it mean?

She resolved to see this course through to its logical end, hoping to find out. With that in mind, she stepped closer, right into his arms. Looping her hands around his neck, she pressed her body against his.

"I feel like that too," she whispered to him, right before she reached up and matched her lips to his.

The kiss took off from there, starting gently and turning into a tempest of need and longing. Sven's hands came around her body, shaping and molding her form to his. She was caught up in the storm, tossed on the waves of their shared desire, swept away on a spiral of passion that rose higher and higher. It was a doozy of a kiss. Like nothing she'd ever experienced before.

And then, she was flying, floating in his arms, moving without effort. Belatedly, she realized he'd picked her up. His strength made her tingle in appreciation as he carried her deeper into his lair. She didn't really care where he was taking them—as long as their destination contained a bed or some other suitable surface on which to explore this combustible attraction between them.

She heard a door open, then he was

lowering her onto her back as he broke the kiss to stare down at her. His eyes were like molten flames, and her cold saltwater heart wanted to leap into the fire with him. Only with him.

That was the mer side talking, coming alive for a man as it never had before. Sirena had somehow known there was something different about Sven from the moment they met. He stirred not only her human passions, but also the deep, dark mer side of her nature that was slow to act and somewhat aloof. Any man who could do that was dangerous, indeed.

"Are you sure?" was all he said, but she understood the nuance of his tone.

If she agreed to this, then she agreed to more than just this one night. It might not be forever, but from the way they sparked off each other every time they touched, it could take a while to slake the thirst that had sprung up between them.

"I'm sure."

Her words were low and intimate...just between them...just like this magical night and whatever would come after. Her people, his people—they didn't have a say in this. The attraction between them was bigger than judgments and opinions. It was something private, something almost…sacred.

And that's when it hit her. This could be something even more special than she'd thought. It was just possible that Sven was her mate. She wasn't sure, but everything that had happened between them had led to this moment, to this revelation that she was looking at more than what she'd thought would be a temporary relationship at best. This could be for life.

But the answer to his question wouldn't change. She was sure about wanting him. She was sure about tonight. What came after… Well, that was in the hands of the Goddess.

When he still didn't move closer, she took action. He seemed to be waiting for more than just her verbal agreement, so she decided to show him that she wanted him in ways he couldn't ignore. Using her lower body strength, she pushed up and over, rolling him beneath her.

She wouldn't have been able to do it if he hadn't let her, but he was smiling and watching her carefully, as if willing to play along in whatever she wanted. The feeling of power made her laugh. She felt like Venus rising from the waves...only with too much fabric still on her body.

Well, that was easily remedied. Sirena straddled Sven's hips, rising above him while she stretched, removing the shirt she'd put on earlier in the day. It was stretchy and soft and came off with a loving caress of fabric over her arms that made her shiver as she bared herself to him.

Her scales didn't hide her femininity now. She was purely human...soft and vulnerable. Bare from the waist up, she sat back and watched Sven's fascination with her flesh, loving the desire she saw in his eyes. Reaching for his hands, she intertwined their fingers for a moment, lifting his hands upward, then untangling them while she placed his palms over her breasts.

Warm, strong hands learned the shape of her body. His touch was tender, but firm, exploratory but knowing. He tried different ways to touch her, studying her response, taking time to figure out what she liked. She could appreciate his care, but the way he was touching her was driving the flames higher. She couldn't take much more without exploding. She had to do something.

Wiggling against the hard rod of his cock

through their clothing, she settled over him in a way guaranteed to drive her out of her mind if they didn't get rid of the fabric soon. She decided to do something about it. She unbuttoned his shirt and pushed it aside, down over his massive shoulders, exposing a muscled torso that she could spend a few idyllic hours licking...later.

Right now, she wanted more. She slid down his legs, and he sat up as she moved lower, seeming unwilling to let her go completely out of his reach. He continued to stroke her body as she set to work on removing his pants. The belt was easy, but the zipper was a bit stubborn—coupled with the fact that she was trying to be careful. She didn't want to unman him before he got a chance to show her just how talented he was with that big dick pressing right up against his fly.

When she finally freed him, he groaned in appreciation as she wrapped her hand around him. He was a big man, and she looked forward to learning how they would fit together. For now, though, she wanted to explore more, but he forestalled what she planned next by lifting her by the arms, placing her beneath him on the mattress.

The show of strength made her cream her panties. Speaking of which…she wanted them gone. As if he heard her thoughts, Sven took a moment to meet her gaze before lowering her stretchy pants and panties all in one go. He slid them all the way off, following the slow path of the fabric with his hands, stroking her from hip to ankle and back again in a way that made her shiver.

When he moved back up her body, he spread her legs wide before him, exposing her. This was the moment when she knew she trusted him beyond all doubt. Sven had seen her through one of the worst events of her life, but he wasn't just someone who could be trusted to help her when she was down. No, Sven was someone she could trust with her innermost secrets, her hopes, her dreams, her passion and…her heart?

She didn't have time to examine that thought further because he lowered his lips to kiss a trail from her belly button down to the apex of her thighs, using his tongue in amazingly expert ways to bring her to a sharp, fast climax. Sweet Mother of All! That was unexpected.

She was still shaking when he kissed his way up her body, stalking forward over her like the predator he was. She cupped his face, loving the feel of his pale golden beard stubble beneath her hands as she pulled him to her for a deep, soul-shattering kiss.

"I can't wait, Sirena. I thought I could, but..." he whispered against her lips before diving deep for another lingering kiss. When they came up for air again, they were both breathing harder than ever. "You do things to me, woman." His tone was exasperated but teasing, and she loved that he could bring fun into these tense moments. Everything with Sven was brighter. He just made her happy, on so many levels.

"I want to do a lot of things to you, doctor, but right now, I don't want to wait either." She slid her body downward, seeking the hard shaft that was rubbing against her thigh. "I want you now, Sven. Don't make me beg."

He lifted his head to stare down into her eyes. "I would never. Well, not for real." His smile sent a little thrum of pleasure through her. "Your wish is my command, princess."

"Then, do me hard, bear-man. Make me yours."

Where were those words coming from? Some little hussy must've taken up residence in her brain because Sirena had never said such things aloud before. She might've thought them, but she'd been too reserved to actually *say* anything to any of her past lovers. Not that there had been all that many.

All thought fled as Sven joined their bodies together in one long, glorious slide that took him inside and filled her completely. They were a match. A perfect match, if what she was feeling held true. Damn. He felt really good inside her.

He started moving, and all hell broke loose—in the best possible sense. He pushed into her deep, then retreated, taking part of her soul into his and returning it with part of his. He took and gave with equal measure, meeting and receding, like the waves on the shore. First, a gentle lapping of wavelets, then a set of breakers, and then, the tempest, followed by the tsunami of pleasure that made her scream his name.

It seemed like only moments, but he had built the pleasure over time so that, when she finally came, the explosion was so great she might've blacked out for a few moments. She would never be sure. The only thing she knew for certain was that Sven held her throughout. Was with her throughout. He was her safe harbor in the storm. He was both the gale itself and the gentle sunshine after.

He held her in his arms as she shook with rapture, then as her shaking dissipated into minor quivers of the memory of bliss, he held her still. It was as if he didn't ever want to let her go, and she felt the same in that moment. That shared time of ecstasy fulfilled and lifelong memories made. Their first time together had been monumental, and she never wanted it to end.

Sven shifted them so that they lay side by side, his arm still around her as they both tried to calm their breathing. Her body was slick with sweat and...other things. A dip in the ocean would clean her right up, but she couldn't move. She never wanted to leave Sven's side.

Ever.

Whoa. Serious thoughts. Too serious for right now. Now was time to float and enjoy the sensations that had been all too fleeting and far between in her life. Of course, she'd never had sex like this before. Sven was unparalleled in her limited experience, and now that she'd had him once, she hoped they would have many more encounters. Many, *many* more.

She might have drifted for a time, sleeping in Sven's embrace. When she woke, she was alone in the bed, but she didn't think too much time had passed. It was still dark outside the windows she spotted on the far side of the room.

If the main area of the house was the sea, the bedroom was the beach. Sandy tans and woody browns dominated, with touches of green and a few splashes of complementary colors. Sven's house was the next best thing to being outdoors, and she loved every last detail of it.

"Sorry," Sven said, coming back into the room from a doorway she hadn't noticed before. It looked like his bathroom. "I didn't mean to wake you."

"It's okay." She sat up in the bed, taking the sheet he must've put over her along with her, a bit shy now that they'd made love.

He sat on her side of the bed, facing her. "I have to apologize again. I didn't use protection. You...overwhelmed me a bit, Sirena. I'm sorry."

She did some mental math and smiled. "It's okay. My mer side changes things a bit for my human side in that respect. I've been wearing my scales for long enough this time that we should be okay for a while. I probably won't be back on a human schedule for a month or two considering how long I've been in the ocean this trip."

"Really? That's kind of fascinating. I don't know of any other shifter that has that sort of issue." He was sounding like a doctor again, but she didn't mind. That doctor's mind was a part of him, just like his polar bear fur.

"Hmm. I'll let you in on more mermaid secrets, in time, but first, you should probably make love to me again. Just to make sure that first time wasn't a fluke." She teased him, loving the way he went from cerebral to sexy in no time flat. He was a complicated man, but she'd enjoy spending time learning all his edges and angles. And most especially his hard spots…

CHAPTER THIRTEEN

Invigorated from their night of lovemaking and the sweet friction of their magic energizing them both, Sirena left Sven's house with him the next morning. They were headed to the clinic for a while. He had a patient to see, and she wanted to get her stuff.

Leaving him in his office with a kiss, she went to the room she'd been using in the clinic to pack up the few items that she might want to keep. A toothbrush, toothpaste, a few other toiletries and some fuzzy socks Sven had given her from the stock he kept on hand in the clinic. There wasn't much, but then, she didn't have much here in Grizzly Cove with her. She'd have to make arrangements for some of the items she'd had placed in storage sent, but that would take a few days.

Last night had been amazing, and for the foreseeable future, at least, she'd be staying at Sven's place. She had to smile when she thought of it. He'd turned out to be a man of hidden talents. She felt herself blushing as she thought about some of the naughtier hidden talents he'd shown her last night. The evening had certainly been…educational.

"Are you involved with the polar bear now, Sirena?" Beth's accusing voice came to Sirena from the doorway.

She'd been so lost in thought Sirena hadn't heard her friend's approach. Beth entered the small room, followed by the rest of the hunting party. Jetty, Grace, Janice and Marla filed in, the last one shutting the door behind them.

"What is this? Some kind of ambush?" Sirena asked, only half joking.

Beth looked angry, while the others looked sort of mildly amused. Sirena wasn't sure exactly what was going on, but one thing was clear—her friends were ganging up on her for some reason, and she suspected the reason was over six feet tall and in his office a short distance away at the moment.

"Call it an intervention," Beth replied stiffly.

She wasn't the easiest personality to get along with, but under the waves, they'd been able to coexist peacefully. Sirena wasn't sure that would hold true while on land. This, in fact, might be the first big test as to whether Sirena could deal with Beth's suspicious nature out of the ocean. The woman had issues. Many unresolved issues that Sirena didn't know all that much about, sadly.

"You can't lead our hunting party while you're cavorting around with a polar bear," Beth stated baldly.

"Says who?" Sirena countered, looking at each one of her friends in turn.

Jetty plopped down onto the empty bed and folded her arms. "Don't look at me. I like the bears."

"Me too," Grace agreed, sitting down next to Jetty. Both women were mated to bear shifters and were very happy.

Beth shook her head at the seated women. "I expected as much from you two. You've gone native since coming ashore, but we're mer. We don't belong with land shifters."

"I repeat: Says who?" Sirena said again.

Beth sputtered for a moment. "It— It goes against nature—" she began, but Jetty cut her off.

"Honey, my mating is solid. Goddess-blessed. You can't get more natural than that. You're the one who's misinformed here, Beth. You should get your facts straight before you start throwing around accusations."

"Goddess-blessed?" Beth sounded outraged. "How can you even say that? How do you know?"

"Beth," Grace said in a softer tone, "if you were mated, you'd understand."

"Oh, don't pull that on me. I won't get tangled up with one of those hairy beasts just to test your theory. I think you're all delusional!"

Jetty just shook her head. "We're not asking you to bed a bear shifter. You wouldn't understand unless you somehow happened to find your perfect mate. Like we did." Jetty nudged Grace with her elbow.

"Finding your mate is something special," Grace picked up the thread of her friend's words. "If you're ever blessed to discover your mate, you'll understand how wrong you are to say that some of us don't belong with some of the bears. It was meant to be, or Jetty and I wouldn't be sitting here, smugly happy that we've found our other halves." Grace smiled, turning her gaze to Sirena. "Like I think maybe Sirena has too."

"So what do you say, Sirena?" Jetty prompted. "Is Sven your mate?"

Sirena's jaw dropped open, and she was searching for an answer when the door opened abruptly. There was Sven, framed in the doorway, his gaze going quickly over the scene in the small room.

"Is this a private party or can anyone join?" he asked, the growl of the bear audible in his voice. He didn't wait for an answer, but moved into the room, taking up all the remaining space, until he was able to station himself at Sirena's side. His arm came around her waist as he nuzzled close to whisper in her ear. "Are you all right?"

She patted his hand. "It's okay. We were just talking."

"Actually, we were just discussing the future of our hunting party," Beth said in a frosty tone. "Nothing to concern you, bear."

Sven's muscles tensed, and she clutched

at his arm to keep him from going after Beth. Not that she really thought he would get violent in such a confined space, but she didn't know him as well as she would in say…fifty or sixty years, so she wasn't taking any chances.

"Everything to do with Sirena is my concern, Beth," he said, that growl in his voice growing deeper, turning Sirena on at a most inappropriate time.

"Why's that?" Jetty asked him with a broad grin on her face.

"Because she's my mate," Sven answered simply, flooring Sirena with his public declaration.

"That's all I needed to hear," Jetty said, smiling from ear to ear as she jumped off the bed and headed for the door, sweeping her arms out to guide the others out before her. "Come on, ladies, it's time to leave these two alone for a bit."

Grace followed Jetty, turning back only once to smile at Sirena and whisper. "Congratulations, you two!"

Beth kept looking back, but Jetty tugged her out of the room rather forcefully, before she could say anything else. It was clear Beth was going to be a problem, but for now, her friends would deal with it while Sirena dealt with the new man in her life. Her *mate*.

He'd never said *that* before. Then again, neither had she. Oh, she'd been thinking about it a bit, but hadn't really dared dream he was experiencing the same things she was feeling. Maybe she should have had more faith in the Goddess who seemed to have brought them together.

Sirena turned to face Sven, putting herself more firmly into his embrace. "So. Mates, huh?" she challenged him with a smile on her face and a tilt of her head.

"Mates," he confirmed. "If you'll have me."

Was that uncertainty on his handsome face?

"I think I can put up with you, if you'll put up with me needing to traipse off into the ocean every once in a while." She put both hands on his chest, loving the warmth of him. "It won't be for long, and I promise not to leave you flat with no explanations, but every once in a while, the mer side needs to get back in touch with the ocean depths for a few days. Every few years or so."

"Years?" Sven looked surprised. "I can live with a few days every few years. I can live with whatever you need to do to keep both sides of your nature in good shape, Sirena. Your happiness is my number one goal now that I've found you. My bear side will want to watch over you and protect you. He'll want to swim with you, if you'll let him, and here in the cove, we can do that just about whenever we want. Just don't send him—us—me—away. I love you, Sirena."

He dipped his head, and she met him halfway in a kiss that spoke of love and longing, acceptance and coming home. When they finally came up for air, she smiled at him, her heart beating in time with his.

"I love you too."

"Let's blow this popsicle stand," he muttered, making her laugh at the odd expression as he swept her up into his arms. "We've got better things to be doing, in more private places."

He didn't wait for her to answer through her laughter. He just walked out of the clinic, still holding her in his arms. He was in such a rush they actually passed her friends in the parking lot. Grace and Jetty whistled. and some of the others offered teasing advice and catcalls as Sven stormed across the parking lot and up the mostly hidden path to his home. Sirena giggled like a schoolgirl all the way, her heart lighter than it had been since childhood.

Sven had brought the magic back to her life. The joy. The spontaneous happiness. He was incredible—and perfect for her. The Goddess did, indeed, know what She was doing when She had paired them up.

They made love slower this time. The urgency of the night before had waned in the morning light, allowing them to enjoy each other in a more leisurely way. Sven was amazingly tender and thoughtful, and Sirena was swept up in the storm of passion he created. He was the whirlwind, and she clung to him, knowing he would take her places she otherwise would never have imagined.

Everything was fresh and new with Sven. Everything was…perfect.

"I still can't quite believe you're my mate," she whispered to him in the lull between bouts of the most incredible lovemaking she'd ever experienced.

He leaned up on one elbow to look down at her as she rested at his side in the beach-like bedroom she loved. He was frowning, and she was sorry she'd put that look on his face at a time that should only be filled with wonder and smiles.

"You're not sure about us?" he asked, all too serious.

"No, I'm sure." She was quick to reassure him. "I'm just...flabbergasted, I guess. I thought I was going to live my life alone. I'd given up on love everlasting and perfect mates. I thought it was all a fairytale that only came true for other people. I can't believe you're here, with me. It feels like a dream." She reached up and cupped his cheek, seeking the solidity of him, reassuring herself she really wasn't dreaming. "The best possible dream."

"A dream made reality," he said, turning his face in her palm to place a kiss there, his good humor restored.

When he turned back, he met her gaze as her hand dropped, the blue of his eyes was lovely to behold, though she'd never say that to him in exactly those words. She'd come up with something more manly and dignified to describe the aquatic blueness of his gaze if the need ever arose.

"I'd all but given up too. I mean, I know we started this town as a way to gather shifters together, in hopes that some of us could find mates and settle down, but I honestly thought that was for the other guys. I figured I'd grow old here, among friends, where I'm needed, but that I'd be alone. I thought maybe I'd use my medical degree to help take care of my friends and their families while I remained a bachelor. I just didn't think there was a woman out there for me."

"You were looking in the wrong species. There wasn't a female bear shifter out there for you. You had to wait for the mer to rise from the sea. Just like I did." She nodded in affirmation of her own little pet theory. "Until everything came together here in the cove—my people and your people and the magic that draws us and binds us—it wasn't possible. But I believe now that it was all meant to be." She tilted her head, thinking. "Although I guess I'll ask Mrs. Legine what she thinks when I get a chance. She's a priestess, after all. Maybe she'd know. Or perhaps your friend, Gus."

"They're both spooky, that's for sure. You know, I heard Mrs. L is already badgering poor Mellie about her potions?"

"Potions?" It seemed so odd to be talking about witches and potions, priestesses and magic here on land with her polar bear-shifter lover.

"You've met Mellie and Urse, the *strega* sisters. Well, Urse is the one who cast the spells that protect the cove. That's her thing. She spell-casts. But her sister does potions, and she's been working on something big for a while now. She's waiting for just the right formula, or recipe, or whatever you'd call it, and the right time. Something to do with the cycles of the moon, I think."

"You're kidding. Really?" She'd never dealt with magic users of any kind, so this was all new territory to her.

"I wouldn't be surprised if Mellie can expand on her sister's protections, and Mrs. L seems determined to help, from all accounts. Plus, John has already called for some other specialist help. He's got contacts all over, and he's called in a few favors on this since it's such a big problem affecting so many. Not just shifters, but sea life in general. And after Mrs. L's discoveries and revelations, it's more important than ever to shut the leviathan down once and for all."

Sirena thought about that. The threat of the leviathan producing offspring that were at home, so to speak, in this realm was very real and extremely troubling. She'd seen that thing in action. She'd been the chew toy of one of its smaller fellows and had nearly died. She couldn't even imagine what the ocean would be like with creatures like that everywhere. It wouldn't be safe for mer, or any sort of magical being. And the leviathan ate regular fish too. As massive as it was, it ate a *lot*.

Already they'd noticed the impact its presence had on their hunting. If there were more leviathans out there, the fish populations would be decimated. She could easily see the creature attacking human vessels. Fishermen wouldn't be safe. Eventually, the humans would learn there was something going on in the oceans, and from there, it wouldn't be hard to see the secret of magic and magical beings like shifters and vampires coming out.

She truly feared what would happen if the humans figured out Others had been living among them. The backlash could be catastrophic. Even with all their magic, magical folk were outnumbered many times over, and humans had strength in numbers. If her kind were hunted by humans on land while leviathans overran the seas, no corner of the Earth would be safe.

Sirena rolled toward him, and Sven laid back, making room for her to cuddle against his side. She put her arm over his chest, needing to feel the solidity of him. He made her feel safe, even with such dire thoughts crossing her mind.

"I don't know what's going to happen with my hunting party. Three of us are mated now, and hunters are usually single. Plus, Beth seems to have a problem." Sirena didn't want to think about her friend's rotten attitude when there were bigger fish to chase, but it was a consideration. "The thing is, Sven..." She wasn't sure how this was going to go down, but she hoped he'd understand. "I'm a hunter. Regardless of what happened to me with the leviathan, I'm one of the best. That's why I was put in charge of the hunting party. We've been the top providers for our pod for years, and we teach the others how to work as a unit. I'm one of the leaders of my pod, and I can't sit on the sidelines when we're all in danger."

Sven hugged her closer for a moment and kissed the top of her head. Her cheek was against his chest, her ear pressed to the reassuring beat of his heart.

"I don't expect you to give up your position with your people, sweetheart. The only thing I ask is that you not put yourself at unnecessary risk and that, when possible, we hunt together. After all, I was a Special Forces soldier for longer than you've probably been alive. I know a thing or two about combat. I may be a doctor, and you've only ever seen me putting folks back together, but I'm also a bear. I know all there is to know about tearing things apart too."

She liked the edge of ferocity in his voice. She liked the growl in his chest. He was reminding her that, though he was gentle with her, he could be even scarier than she realized. Somehow, that made her feel better. Safer. As if nothing could hurt them—as long as they were together.

She lifted her head to meet his gaze. "I think I can live with that." She thought again about her friends. "Besides, I don't think my hunting party is going to survive all this upheaval intact. Maybe it's time to reformulate the squad. Jetty used to be my second, but she's already told me she's retiring for now. She's enjoying being newly mated and wants to spend time with her husband. Grace will probably say the same once she works up the courage to talk to me about it."

"So that leaves you two mermaids down," Sven observed.

"Three, probably, with Beth mad at me and somehow prejudiced against bears. I have no idea where that came from. She's usually very quiet and steadfast."

Sven shook his head, smiling. "It's always the quiet ones."

Sirena pushed at his shoulder playfully. "I think she's just mixed up. Probably a little scared about all the changes. I don't think she's the kind of person who handles change well. She'll settle down in time."

"Settle down? That's a funny choice of words. Do you want her to find a nice bear shifter to mate with?" Sven asked, pointing out something she must've been thinking subconsciously.

"You know? I guess I do. I want all my friends to find a mate, and the happiness I have." She kissed his chest gently, her eyes misting with emotion. "I wasn't sure I'd ever find a man to spend my life with. When I saw Jetty and Grace, I was happy for them, but a bit jealous too, if I'm being honest. Now that I have you, I feel…complete…for the first time in a very long time. I want all my friends—even Beth—to find what I have. They deserve happiness too."

"I can see why you were chosen to lead the hunting party. You love your people, like any good leader should." Sven sat up, lifting her with him so that he could take her into his arms and place a loving kiss on her lips.

They didn't speak again for some time. Instead, they communicated by touch and sensation. Sven's talented hands brought her to a state where she was just about going out of her mind with want. Then, he joined their bodies together, taking them on the journey to the stars and back, while he held her secure in his embrace.

Sven's touch had healed her in so many ways, and he continued to show her new delights and temptations. Sirena saw a future spread before her filled with love and passion, tenderness and healing for her body as well as her soul. Her man was a complex mixture of savage bear instincts and a gentle human heart that wanted to help those in pain.

She'd come to him injured and near death, and he'd saved her and given her a new chance at life. He'd also given her a love she never could have imagined and had given up hoping to find. It had all happened so fast, but that's how it was when you found your destiny—or so the legends said.

Sirena knew there would be tough times and battles ahead, but she also felt that, with Sven by her side, she could face whatever came. They were a team now, and heaven help anything or anyone that stood against them.

EPILOGUE

John hung up the phone and sighed. He'd just spoken to the Kinkaid Alpha—a billionaire lion shifter who led a rather odd mixture of land and sea shifters. The complicated lineage had led the Kinkaids from Ireland to Africa and then to America, where the mixed up Clan now kept its headquarters. The Kinkaids were best known for their lions, but they also laid claim to a very magical selkie heritage. It was the selkies John needed to consult, but to do that, he had to gain agreement from the Alpha—a badass lion with a reputation for being sharp in his business dealings and fair with his people.

In the end, it had been surprisingly simple to get Samson Kinkaid to agree to ask one of his people to come out and consult on their little leviathan problem. Turns out, the lion Alpha knew more about the leviathan than John had expected. Seems they'd run into the issue themselves a short while back, in the Atlantic. That the leviathan had moved to the Pacific was news to Kinkaid, but he was quick to offer help once he realized the creature had, indeed, jumped oceans.

At least one selkie—a seal shifter out of Irish legends—was already en route, with the possibility of more on the way. John had the dubious task of keeping the Kinkaid representative safe while in his domain. He wanted selkie input on the leviathan problem, but he didn't want anyone harmed.

He especially didn't want any of Kinkaid's people harmed while in John's territory. The last thing he wanted was to piss off the lions.

It looked like interesting times were ahead for the residents of Grizzly Cove. For one thing, John wasn't sure how the mer were going to get along with the selkies. He hadn't really had time to run this idea past Nansee yet. When he'd put the call in to Kinkaid, he'd had to wait for a reply, since the lion

Alpha had been off the grid.

John had placed that first call weeks ago and, frankly, had forgotten all about it in light of the arrival of the mer in the cove. Apparently, Kinkaid was back in coms range now and had just called back. The fact that Kinkaid might go off-grid again at any moment had left John no time to consult with the mer leader.

He sighed. He was the Alpha, and it was on his head. He only hoped the introduction of yet another new shifter species into the small town wouldn't cause more problems than it could potentially solve. Still, he had to admit, they needed all hands on deck to battle the leviathan, and he'd take any assistance that was offered. If that meant the water shifters would have to figure out the dominance chain, then so be it.

With the leviathan stalking their shores, they needed all the help they could get.

# # #

ABOUT THE AUTHOR

Bianca D'Arc has run a laboratory, climbed the corporate ladder in the shark-infested streets of lower Manhattan, studied and taught martial arts, and earned the right to put a whole bunch of letters after her name, but she's always enjoyed writing more than any of her other pursuits. She grew up and still lives on Long Island, where she keeps busy with an extensive garden, several aquariums full of very demanding fish, and writing her favorite genres of paranormal, fantasy and sci-fi romance.

Bianca loves to hear from readers and can be reached via Facebook (BiancaDArcAuthor) or through the various links on her website.

WELCOME TO THE D'ARC SIDE...
WWW.BIANCADARC.COM

OTHER BOOKS
BY BIANCA D'ARC

Paranormal Romance

Brotherhood of Blood
One & Only
Rare Vintage
Phantom Desires
Sweeter Than Wine
Forever Valentine
Wolf Hills*
Wolf Quest

Tales of the Were
Lords of the Were
Inferno
Rocky
Slade

Tales of the Were ~ Redstone Clan
The Purrfect Stranger
Grif
Red
Magnus
Bobcat
Matt

Epic Fantasy Erotic Romance

Dragon Knights
Maiden Flight*
The Dragon Healer
Border Lair

Dragon Knights
(continued)
Master at Arms
The Ice Dragon**
Prince of Spies***
Wings of Change
FireDrake
Dragon Storm
Keeper of the Flame
Hidden Dragons
The Sea Captain's Daughter Trilogy
Book 1: Sea Dragon
Book 2: Dragon Fire
Book 3: Dragon Mates

Science Fiction Romance

StarLords
Hidden Talent
Talent For Trouble
Shy Talent

Jit'Suku Chronicles ~ Arcana
King of Swords
King of Cups
King of Clubs
King of Stars
End of the Line
Diva

Jit'Suku Chronicles ~ Sons of Amber
Angel in the Badlands
Master of Her Heart

Futuristic Erotic Romance

Resonance Mates
Hara's Legacy**
Davin's Quest
Jaci's Experiment
Grady's Awakening
Harry's Sacrifice

* RT Book Reviews Awards Nominee
** EPPIE Award Winner
*** CAPA Award Winner

WWW.BIANCADARC.COM

Made in the USA
San Bernardino, CA
07 February 2017